LOVE'S JOURNEY HOME

LOVE'S JOURNEY HOME

JULIE COULTER BELLON

STONE
HALL
BOOKS

ALSO BY JULIE COULTER BELLON

CANADIAN SPY SERIES

Through Love's Trials

On the Edge

Time Will Tell

THE VETERAN'S CLUB REGENCY SERIES

The Marquess Meets His Match

The Viscount's Vow

The Highlander's Hidden Heart

DOCTORS AND DANGER SERIES

All's Fair

Dangerous Connections

Ribbon of Darkness

THE HOSTAGE NEGOTIATION SERIES

All Fall Down (Hostage Negotiation #1)

Falling Slowly (Hostage Negotiation #1.5)

Ashes Ashes (Hostage Negotiation #2)

From the Ashes (Hostage Negotiation #2.5)

Pocket Full of Posies (Hostage Negotiation #3)

Forget Me Not (Hostage Negotiation #3.5)

Ring Around the Rosie (Hostage Negotiation #4)

THE GRIFFIN FORCE SERIES

The Captive (Griffin Force #1)

The Captain (Griffin Force #2)

The Capture (Griffin Force #3)

Second Look (Griffin Force #4)

Second Chance (Griffin Force #5)

THE LINCOLN LOVE STORIES SERIES

Love's Broken Road

Love's Journey Home

ACKNOWLEDGMENTS

I have so many people to thank who helped this book see the light of day after an incredible amount of setbacks that made me wonder if it would ever happen!

Wendy Jurgens and Robyn Wood let me interview them for hours and answered a thousand questions for me so I could make my characters as realistic as possible. Thank you!

Jeni Roberts, Jodi Bezzant, Robyn Wood, and Jon Spell read the manuscript in several different stages and offered so many helpful suggestions and encouragement. It probably would still be sitting in a computer file unfinished without them. Thank you!

My critique partner, Annette Lyon, has been the biggest cheerleader as I've tried my hand at romance. I've laughed and cried with her as this book went through revision after revision. Her support meant the world to me. Thank you!

But my biggest thanks and all my love goes to my family. I

couldn't do this without them and it wouldn't mean much unless I could share it with them. They make it all worth it. Love you!

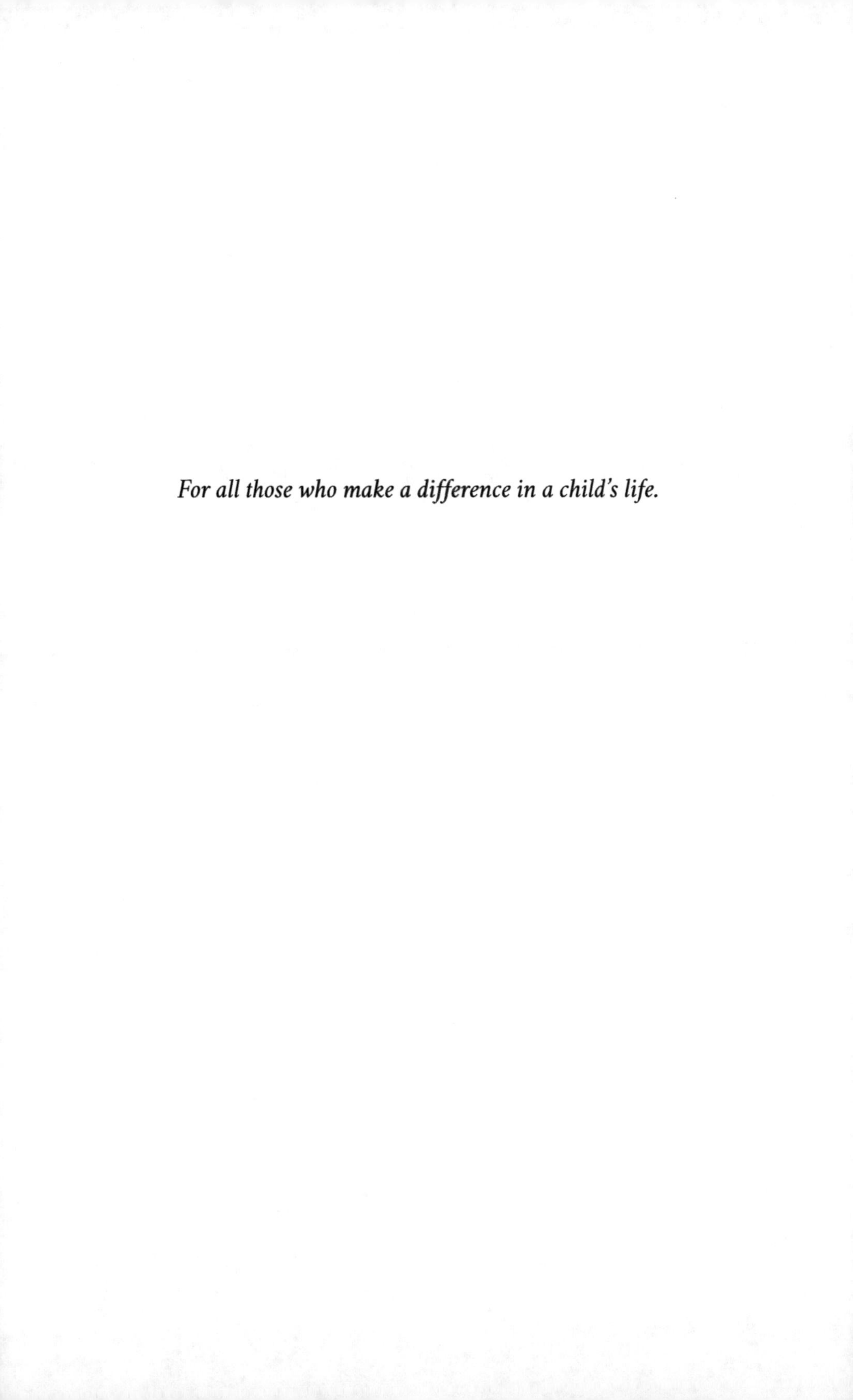

For all those who make a difference in a child's life.

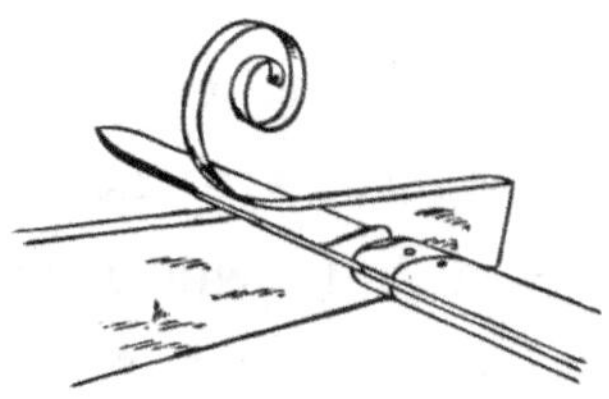

Sometimes helping out a friend didn't give the warm fuzzy feelings everyone talked about.

Mick Donovan stood behind the new waitress from Rosie's restaurant, holding her hair away from her face while she vomited on a bush out back. It was late, and Mick could only see shadows cast from the weak flickers of a lone streetlight. If they'd been out front, there would have been plenty of light from the lampposts strategically placed on Lincoln's Main Street, but there would also be a crowd of witnesses waiting to be seated for dinner.

After a few seconds of silence, when the worst of it was over, he quietly asked, "You okay? Your name's Adrienne, right?"

She straightened and wiped her mouth on the back of her hand. Peering up at him, she blinked a few times, as if he weren't in focus. "Yeah. Thanks." Giving him a drunken smile, she took a step and wobbled. Mick grabbed her elbow to steady her. She held on tight, as if he were a lifeline, her nails digging into his arm. "I don't think I caught your name."

"Mick Donovan. I'm friends with Taunya, remember?" He guided her toward his car, hoping she'd emptied her stomach enough that he wouldn't have to clean his seats later. "She asked me to take you home."

"I shouldn't have come into work, but I was so hungry. I just needed a little pick me up." She looked at him owlishly. Her mascara had run, leaving black smudges on her cheeks, giving her the appearance of a child who'd been in her mother's makeup. "You understand that, right? I mean, Tim can't fire me for asking for food, can he?"

Tim was the manager of Rosie's, the only non-fast food restaurant in Lincoln, and he ran a tight ship with his staff. She very well could get fired, but Mick didn't want to mention that to her right now. "That's why Taunya asked me to take you home. So Tim didn't see you." He held up the paper bag in his hand. "She even sent you with some takeout. For later. When you feel better."

"Taunya's the best," Adrienne said, glancing back at the employee entrance. Mick silently agreed. She was the kind of person anyone would be lucky to know.

He'd met Taunya at the diner six months ago and he'd started to come in when he knew she'd be waitressing. She had a great smile to go along with her long legs and sunshine-blonde hair. But after they'd gone out a few times, he did what he always had and broke it off. She was looking to settle down and have a family, but Mick knew he would never be that guy, so he'd backed away.

They'd remained friends, though, and he was glad about

that. A man couldn't have too many friends, especially ones with good hearts—except when that good-hearted person involved him with someone throwing up. He'd never had a particularly strong stomach, and with fresh vomit on his shoes, he was starting to feel nauseated. Hopefully he wouldn't regret being a good friend and doing Taunya a favor tonight.

"I'm going to put you in my car. Tell me if you feel sick so I can pull over, okay?" He helped her in and sighed as he shut the door to his Mustang. Luckily, they didn't have far to go to get to her apartment building.

Mick went around to the other side of the car and got in, immediately cracking all the windows so he could breathe in some of the crisp October air. Adrienne's eyes were closed, and her head was against the window. "You good?" he asked, wanting to double-check the state of her stomach.

She nodded briefly, as if it was too much effort to do more than that. "Just need to go home."

Mick started the car and the engine purred to life. "If I didn't know the Lincoln police had a speed trap on the street that goes up to your house, I'd get you there in two minutes flat."

"This is a Mustang, isn't it?" She opened one eye and looked at him. "Zero to sixty in seven seconds."

Mick gave a low chuckle. He'd worked hard to get his Mustang and was proud of it. "Yeah. Which doesn't do me much good in Lincoln. But get me out on the salt flats, and I can practically fly in this baby." He patted the dash, feeling the purr of the engine under his fingers. "Don't worry, we'll get you home in no time, though."

He pulled out onto the street and headed toward the row of

duplexes on the south side of town. Lincoln wasn't big, and Adrienne lived with a few other waitresses at Blue Gables Townhomes. Each duplex had a bright blue roof, so while it was a bit on the ugly side, at least it was easy to find.

When he pulled up outside the duplex at the end of the street, a soft snore came out of Adrienne's mouth, and he realized she was sleeping. *Better than throwing up.*

"Hey." He lightly touched her shoulder, noticing how threadbare her t-shirt was. "You're home."

She lifted her head and blinked a few times, looking around to get her bearings. "What?"

"You're home." He smiled, and she moved away from him, her brow furrowed as if she was trying to remember who he was. "I'm Taunya's friend, Mick. She was worried Tim would see you at the restaurant when you weren't . . . at your best." Drunk and disorderly was more like it. Taunya had escorted her out of the kitchen while Adrienne had still been demanding two steaks and some shrimp.

She stared at him, then rubbed her temples. "I wash-sh hungry."

"How much did you have to drink?" Her speech sounded slurred more than sleepy.

"What are you, my mother?" Adrienne straightened and glared at him, fumbling for the door handle. "I'm fine. I just need to get to bed."

"Okay." He wasn't going to argue with her. He opened his door and quickly came around to help her out.

She stumbled a bit and grabbed his arm, but as soon as she was steady, backed away. "Thanks for bringing me home," she said grudgingly, looking up at the ugly blue roof, as if to make sure she really was home.

Mick cupped her elbow, not willing to leave her on the sidewalk when it looked like she was having a hard time taking a few steps. "Taunya wouldn't forgive me if I left you out here. Let me be a gentleman and take you to the door."

"Ooh, a gentleman." Her expression changed from an angry pout to a grin. She leaned in. "I haven't had a gentleman around in a while. Tell me the truth, do you think I'm pretty, Mr. Gentleman?"

Mick groaned inwardly. At the moment, her hair was matted, with a little bit of greenery from the bush tangled in it. Her clothes were disheveled and her makeup smeared. He'd seen her sober, however, and put together. She was a pretty woman when at her best, but that probably wasn't a good thought to share right now. "I think you've had a little too much to drink and you need to sleep it off."

Adrienne pressed against his side. "Do you and Taunya have something going on? Because I won't tell if you won't." She looked up at him and batted her lashes, but whatever effect she was going for got spoiled by the smell of vomit on her breath.

He turned his face slightly away. "There's nothing to tell, and Taunya's a good friend to both of us." He motioned toward her purse. "Can I help you find your keys?"

"All the good guys are taken or not interested," she grumbled as she handed over her purse. "There aren't any gentlemen left."

He rummaged through a pile of receipts until he got to the bottom and felt a key ring. He pulled it out and slid the key into the lock. "I'm sure things will look better when you're sober."

She looked at the open door for a minute, as if she wasn't

quite sure what to do. "I'm a little dizzy," she finally admitted. "Can you help me in?"

He took her arm and walked through the doorway, discreetly pushing away a duffel bag and piles of clothes and shoes strewn about, to clear a path to the living room. She was leaning heavily on him, but when they got near enough, she promptly lay down on the couch and closed her eyes. "I'll just rest here for a minute. You don't have to stay."

Mick stood over her, debating what to do. Should he leave her here in this condition? "Are you sure?"

She kicked off her shoes without opening her eyes, then turned on her side to get comfortable. With as lumpy and worn as the old couch looked, that seemed a feat in itself. "Yeah. Thanks for the ride."

Well, as she'd pointed out, he wasn't her mother, and she seemed to be doing okay now that she was home. Mick turned to leave, but Adrienne sat up straight. "Wait. You didn't bring in my food."

Oh yeah. The food she'd ventured out of the house for that had started this whole mess. He held up a hand. "Don't worry. I'll go get it and put it in your fridge."

She lay back, satisfied, and closed her eyes again. "Thanks."

He jogged back to his car and grabbed the takeout bag. He knew he'd never be able to eat Rosie's famous beef kebabs again. He grimaced and took another deep breath before going back into the apartment. Adrienne was passed out, her bottle-blonde hair sticking up at all angles, the brightness of the bleached yellow a stark contrast against the frayed brown fabric. It was obvious nothing would wake her up, not even food, so Mick decided to make his way to the kitchen.

It was small, the linoleum worn in a few places. She obviously hadn't done dishes for a couple of days. The garbage was overflowing and needed emptied. Mick put the takeout bag in the fridge and decided to at least take care of her garbage before he left. If nothing else, that might improve the odor in her apartment. Mick opened some cupboards and drawers before he found where she kept the bags, and when he looked up, a small boy was in the doorway, his dark hair tousled from sleep.

"Hey," Mick said, covering his surprise. "I'm Mick. What's your name?"

The boy stared at him for an uncomfortably long moment, his brown eyes taking him in, as if Mick was being weighed and evaluated. "I'm Will," he said finally. "Where's my mom?"

"She's in the living room, um, resting." He changed the garbage bag and tied it shut. "She brought some beef kebabs home from Rosie's. Are you hungry?"

Interest lit his eyes, and he nodded. Mick got the takeout bag from the fridge, and when he didn't find any clean plates, he laid a napkin on the table with a kebab in the middle. "Here you go."

The boy eyed him warily, but sat down. He bit into the meat and barely stopped to chew before he put another piece in.

"Whoa, slow down," Mick said, as he sat next to the boy. "You don't want to choke."

Will wiped his mouth on his pajama sleeve, but didn't say anything.

"How old are you?" Mick asked, trying to start a conversation and give himself an excuse to stay longer. Should he leave the boy with his passed-out mother in the other room?

"Seven." He took another bite, but slowly chewed it this time.

"Do you go to Central Elementary?" It was the only elementary school in town, so chances were he went there, but Mick was having a hard time thinking of topics he could talk about with a seven-year-old who was definitely more interested in eating than talking.

"Yeah."

Will finished the kebab in record time and Mick considered offering him the other one, but knew Adrienne would want that for herself.

"You like it there?" Mick asked, trying to draw the boy out.

"It's okay. I like soccer at recess."

That little bit of information felt like a victory of sorts, since Mick had gotten little more than one word answers out of him. "I like soccer, too."

Will started to smile, but caught himself and frowned. "Mrs. Howard said we can't play when it snows, so I hope it never snows."

"Me, too. I have a convertible and like driving with the top down. You can't do that when it's snowing." He balled up the napkin and put it with the empty kebab stick. "Your mom isn't feeling well tonight. She might sleep for a while." How much did the boy know about his mom's condition?

"She sleeps there a lot." Will turned away and headed for the hall. "Night."

He didn't seem upset or scared, as if his mother passing out on the couch was a normal occurrence. It made Mick's heart hurt. Maybe when Adrienne was sober, he could talk to her about getting a babysitter for the boy when she was at work, at least. He shouldn't be here alone.

Mick let himself out and took the garbage to the bin in the back before he got into his car. Debating on whether to leave the boy or stay, he sat staring at the apartment. Will had taken the news of his mother's condition in stride, as if he was used to taking care of himself. Mick decided he'd done what he could for tonight, but his mind couldn't shut down the part of him that remembered himself as a hungry little boy sneaking food whenever his foster mother wasn't looking. No one had cared about him then. Did Will have anyone who truly cared about him?

Mick slowly drove home, pulled into his driveway and turned the car off. The little boy in the kitchen dominated his thoughts, but if he mixed them with his own childhood memories, he knew he wouldn't be able to sleep tonight no matter how hard he tried. Wanting to push it all to the back of his mind, he bypassed the house and went directly to the woodshop he'd built in his garage.

After crossing the large room, he got out his latest project, cradling the piece of wood he'd been working on for months. He'd carved animals and flowers, but this was the first detailed bird he'd attempted. The intricacy of the feathers had been difficult at first, and he'd had to give it all of his focus. Tonight, he knew he didn't have the patience for that kind of detailed work. He'd have to switch to the face.

Once he had his tools in hand and got his rhythm going, his emotions began to calm down. Wood always had that effect on him, which was part of the reason he loved being a woodshop teacher at the high school. He needed that calm to teach teenagers to see the beauty in crafting something with your own hands into a masterpiece.

He lost all track of time until early morning sunlight started to slant through the windows. Mick yawned and looked down at the owl's face, but he didn't see wise eyes. Instead, he saw the eyes of a hungry little boy alone in a house where his mother was passed out on the couch. No matter how many wood pieces he carved, circumstances like last night brought out the feeling of helplessness he'd experienced as a child.

And he knew he needed to have a conversation with Adrienne. Today.

CHAPTER TWO

Olivia Dalton took off her sensible heels and put her feet up on her desk. She'd stayed late last night working on a closing argument and though it was barely past dinner at the moment, she wanted to keep the promise to herself that she wouldn't stay late again tonight. The problem was, the mountain of work in front of her never seemed to get smaller, no matter how early she came into the office or how late she stayed. She needed to go home. Yet the thought of another night eating alone held little appeal.

Jana stuck her head in the door and motioned to the papers on her desk. "You know, none of this is going anywhere. It'll all still be here in the morning." Jana was the office assistant and right hand to all six attorneys in the D.A.'s office. She'd saved Olivia more than once with her research skills, tracking down obscure case law.

"You're right. I know you're right." She let out a sigh, and

Jana came to her desk, a sympathetic smile on her face. "I thought I could make some headway on the Dahlquist case, but I'm spinning my wheels now that Hannah's skipped town. If I could have just gotten that warrant sooner." Olivia bent to put her shoes back on. "We were so close, and I had a hunch I needed to rush on that one. I should have followed it."

"You've had suspects disappear before. Why is this one sticking out to you?" Jana asked as she straightened the files tilting precariously on Olivia's desk.

"I actually think I could have helped her. Or at least helped her kid." The boy's eyes still haunted Olivia. She'd sent Child and Family Services out the day they'd gotten the warrant, but Hannah had already disappeared and taken her son with her. Dealing with drug addicts was part of the job description, and normally Olivia closed off her emotions so she could stay professional, but something about Hannah Dahlquist's boy broke through the barrier.

"You have a tender heart," Jana said, her tight black curls bouncing as she shook her head and walked back toward the door. "That's not good when you're dealing with kids and victims."

"No, it isn't, but getting justice for them helps." And Olivia did her best to make sure her tender heart was protected. If the Dahlquist kid had broken through, she obviously needed to build up immunity to her cases again. "I'm just tired." She reached down to get her purse out of her bottom desk drawer. With one last look to make sure she had everything she needed, she caught up to Jana and they walked down the long hall toward the exit. "Thanks for coming to get me."

The two women walked out to their cars together and said goodbye. Olivia's phone rang as she slid into the driver's seat, and she groaned when she saw the number. David Sullivan. She'd gone out with him twice, but both times she'd noticed him eyeing other women. When he actually slipped his number to a waitress, she'd drawn the line. She'd rather sit home and watch an action movie with no plot but plenty of explosions, than go out with a player who would never be satisfied with just one woman.

She let the phone call go to voicemail, but listened to the message before starting her car. "Hey, Olivia, it's David. My date cancelled last minute so I'm free tonight." His tone lowered, as if he were telling her voicemail a secret. "I know you don't have anything to do besides work, and going out with me is better than staying at the office or being alone, am I right? Call me."

The moment it ended, Olivia deleted the message. Even the sound of his voice made her roll her eyes. How had she ever agreed to even one date with that guy? She wasn't that lonely, was she?

With a sigh, she put her phone down and started the car, slowly driving toward her condo. David's message rang in her ears. *I know you don't have anything to do.* Lately, that was true. She had immersed herself in work for the past year and hadn't left much room for anything else. Life seemed more manageable that way, and a demanding job was a great excuse to say no to a lot of things. Besides, every time she stuck a toe in the dating world, it ended badly. She'd made a rule not to ever go out with other attorneys she might interact with as a D.A., but that limited her potential dates, since she mostly associated with lawyers. Breaking off a workplace romance could sour the work environment, though, and she couldn't risk that.

Without dating attorneys, she didn't date much at all, so her family and friends had started to set her up on blind dates, which led to seeing people like David. The guy who'd told her, "On a scale of one to ten, you're a nine, and I'm the one you need." Oy. That should have been her first clue. Dating him had almost made her want to swear off men forever.

Pressing on the accelerator, she wanted to prove David wrong. She *did* have plans tonight. She was going to visit her brother. That was infinitely better than letting David's prediction come true. Even if they were spur of the moment plans, they were still *plans*. And that counted.

Getting on the freeway, she headed toward Lincoln. It had been a while since she'd seen Drew and Tori. They'd married a few months back and seemed blissfully in love. Sometimes she found it hard to be around them without feeling a whisper of envy, but she was truly happy for them. Her brother had been so lost after his first wife died that Olivia had doubted he'd ever find someone else, but Tori had brought joy back into his life.

As she drove into Lincoln, she passed the high school and saw her brother getting into his car still in the parking lot. What was a high school teacher doing at the school near dinnertime?

She pulled into the spot next to her brother's and rolled down her window. "And you accuse me of constantly working."

Drew turned and smiled when he saw who it was. "Wow, I'm shocked to see you out of the office. Did you get a pass from the principal or something?"

"That would be your department. I don't see principals. Just cranky judges." She grinned. "Actually, if I remember correctly, you're the only one in the family that ever got sent to the principal's office."

Drew laughed and held up a hand. "Okay, okay, I'm sorry I brought it up. It's just been so long since I've seen you that I was caught off guard. I *had* been wondering if maybe you'd been buried under an avalanche of case files and no one had dug you out yet, but here you are."

The image of her desk strewn with files flashed through her mind. If only Drew knew. "Nope, no avalanche, just a girl out on the town."

"Any special plans? Do you have time to grab a bite to eat at Rosie's?" Drew asked, leaning against his car door. His tie was undone, but still hanging around his neck, and his hair was mussed—telltale signs he could probably use a break and some food.

"What about Tori? Is she expecting you?" Olivia didn't want to intrude on anyone else's plans.

"No, I have some time. She took Cal into the city to look for cleats. She's so nervous about him having all the equipment he needs for his first soccer game this weekend. It took her two days to find shin guards that she felt were the perfect fit." He chuckled. "Cal's a trooper, though. He tries every pair on until she's satisfied, and he never complains."

Cal was Tori's son from her first marriage, but Drew loved him as if he were his own. The little boy had fit right into the extended family, too, and Olivia loved being an aunt. Tonight, though, she was glad to have her brother's attention all to herself.

"Rosie's it is, then." She parked her car next to his and got out, locking her doors before getting into Drew's car. "You can drive."

Drew threw his workbag in the back of his car and slid into the driver's seat. Olivia was surprised he waited until they were out of the parking lot before he began his line of questioning. Usually she got the third degree the moment she sat down. Drew had always been a little protective, and even though he was exasperating, she knew he did it because he loved her.

"So tell me, what's the real reason you came down to visit? Is everything okay?" He gave her a sideways glance, and Olivia was glad they were in the car so he couldn't face her head on. He was one of the few people who could usually read her expressions no matter how hard she tried to hide her emotions from him.

"Nothing new," she said finally. "I just missed you."

"Been working a lot?" he asked, as he drove the few blocks to Rosie's. The restaurant parking lot was filled with the dinner rush customers, but Drew found a spot close to the front when someone else was leaving.

"Of course," she said without hesitation. "I love my job."

"Been out on any dates?" He shut the car off and turned to face her.

"A couple." She cringed inwardly, but knew she couldn't bluff. There was just something about growing up with a brother. Even with a perfect poker face, Drew could read all her tells. He'd spot anything less than the truth a mile away.

Please don't ask about them.

"How did they go?" Drew didn't make a move to get out of

the car and instead, settled back into his seat. He wasn't going anywhere until she'd answered.

"Not great." She let out a breath. "On the last one, the guy hit on the waitress right in front of me."

Drew frowned and clenched a fist, but released it slowly. "What was the guy's name?"

"This is why I never tell you about my love life. You go all big brother on me." Olivia laughed and reached for her door handle. It felt good to talk to him and know that he always had her back. "Come on, let's go eat."

They walked inside the crowded restaurant, and after checking in with the hostess, sat down in the waiting area until they were called.

"So how's school going?" Olivia asked, trying to keep the conversation away from her. "Settling into the new routine?" If she could get him talking about his students, she wouldn't have to say another word all night.

"School's fine. We're starting to read Macbeth, and the kids are really enjoying all the mayhem of the story so far." He shifted so he could see her better. "But I want to hear about you. Any big cases you can talk about?"

"Not really." Her eyes had focused on the man sitting at the old-fashioned counter, talking to a waitress. His dark hair was just touching his collar, his jaw showing a little more scruff since she'd seen him last. Memories of going with her brother to chaperone the last high school dance came to mind, along with Drew's warning to avoid his colleague, Mr. Donovan, since he "had the looks and the moves," and wouldn't hesitate to use them on any available woman. "Hey, isn't that the wood-shop teacher from your school? Mick Donovan?"

Drew turned to look and rolled his eyes. "Yeah. I don't know the waitress, though. I bet she just moved here. He can't resist charming the ladies who are new in town and don't know his reputation."

She watched Mick talk to the waitress a little longer. He looked like he'd barely come from the high school as well, wearing a blue button-down shirt and khaki pants. She had to admit, he looked good in blue.

His smile had appealed to her briefly at the dance, as well as the few other times she'd seen him before. But he didn't have any smiles on his face tonight. Whatever Mick and the waitress were discussing, it wasn't flirtatious. "Is he still a player?"

"Does a district attorney have to satisfy the burden of proof?" Drew asked, as their name was called.

Olivia didn't answer and followed the waitress to their table. She passed Mick and glanced at the blonde woman he was talking to. She looked familiar, but was angled away, so that Olivia couldn't be sure. Taking a step forward, she took a closer look. The hair was different, but that was the same face from the case file that had been on her mind for weeks.

"Hannah Dahlquist?" Olivia moved to the counter. "It *is* you. I've been looking everywhere."

For a split second, fear raced across Hannah's face, but then she smoothed her apron down and gave a little laugh. "You're mistaken. My name is Adrienne Jennings."

Olivia's eyebrows drew together. Could she be mistaken? No, there was the distinguishing beauty mark above her top lip and a tiny heart tattoo just below her ear. This was definitely Hannah Dahlquist. That desperate quality still shadowed her eyes. "Hannah, I know it's you. A bad dye job can't hide it."

Hannah's calm slipped for a moment and she glared at Olivia. A few waitresses had slowed down or stopped to listen and even a few diners were turning to look. Covering her anger quickly, Hannah's eyes darted to each person watching them, probably gauging to see if they could help her somehow. Olivia didn't want to cause a scene in the middle of the restaurant, but there wasn't any way she was going to let a suspect go. She pulled out her phone.

Mick put his hand on her arm to stop her call, and he stepped between the women, his mouth in a tight smile. "Wait. Let's back up here a minute. It's good to see you again, Olivia, but as she mentioned, her name is Adrienne." He turned back to the waitress. "This is Olivia Dalton. Since she's a district attorney, she sees a lot of people every day. I'm sure it's easy to mistake a face or a name."

"It's not a mistake." Olivia gritted her teeth as she pulled her arm away. "She's got a rap sheet a mile long."

Hannah was calm again. Too calm. She pressed her palms together. "Like I said, my name is Adrienne. You've got me mixed up with someone else." She looked over her shoulder. "I've got to get back to work. I'll see you later, Mick."

"I don't think so." Olivia started to dial. "You've got a warrant out for your arrest."

Hannah—or Adrienne or whoever she was—didn't waste any time and ran toward the back entrance.

Drew appeared at Olivia's elbow. "What's going on?" He looked curiously between her and Mick.

"I've got to stop her," Olivia said, as she maneuvered around the counter. Dispatch picked up, but with the background noise of the servers and the restaurant, Olivia nearly had to shout into the phone. "This is Olivia Dalton from the D.A.'s office. I'm at Rosie's Grill on Main Street in Lincoln. Hannah Dahlquist is working here, and she has an open warrant out. She's exiting out the back on foot."

Mick was right behind her as they zigzagged around the kitchen workers toward the employee entrance. "Taunya, did you see Adrienne?" he asked, as they stopped in front of a pretty blonde.

"Yeah, she said she was sick again and had to go home. I was surprised you lent her your car keys. I thought the Mustang was sacred and not to be driven by anyone but you."

A glance at Mick's face, coupled with his frantic searching of his pockets, told Olivia that Hannah had stolen his keys. "Give me a description of your Mustang," she said urgently.

"Last year's model. A black convertible." He threw the words over his shoulder as he ran for the back door that led to the parking lot.

Olivia gave the police dispatch the description and hurried outside. They were both in time to see Hannah driving off in Mick's Mustang.

"She's heading north on Main Street," Olivia said into her phone, as she stared at the fast-disappearing car. Mick was frozen beside her, staring at the taillights in disbelief. "Sorry you had to find out about your girlfriend like that."

He didn't deny the relationship, just clenched his jaw and headed back inside the restaurant. Olivia flinched as the door slammed behind him. How involved was he with Hannah? Surely he couldn't be part of the drug operation. If he was, that was one mess he'd have a hard time hiding or getting out of since he lived in a small town and worked at a high school with one of the best gossip chains in the state.

No, unless he was a master of deception, he couldn't be involved. But she'd still have to check.

Sometimes it was hard to be an assistant D.A.

Especially when you knew what was coming next.

CHAPTER THREE

Mick started Taunya's two-door hatchback and pushed the driver's seat all the way back. Pressing the gas pedal, he sped through the quiet streets of Lincoln. Hopefully the Lincoln police hadn't set up their speed traps near the Blue Gables again. But if Adrienne was going to run, she'd probably go home first and pack a few things, and he wanted his car back. He clenched his jaw. When had she stolen his keys? And how did he not notice?

Feeling like an idiot, he drove down Adrienne's street and pulled up to her duplex, but his car wasn't there. Backing out, he decided to circle the block, but didn't see Adrienne or his Mustang. As he scanned the darkness, his headlights picked up a lone child on the swings at the park across the street. The boy ducked his head at the sudden light, but not before Mick recognized him. Will. Hope rose in his chest. Adrienne would come for her son, and when she did, he'd be waiting.

He parked and got out of the car, shoving his hands in his pockets. A breeze picked up, and he wished he'd thought to grab his coat. Keeping his eye on the boy, he walked over and stopped next to his swing. "Hey."

Will's expression was wary as he toed the dirt and moved slightly away from Mick. "Hey."

"I'm looking for your mom. Have you seen her?" Mick leaned against the frame of the swing and glanced around. She wasn't in sight yet.

"No." He looked down and shrugged. "Sometimes she doesn't come home for a long time, though."

Mick's heart cracked a little at the confession, and he squatted down, trying to see Will's eyes. "You come to this park a lot while you wait for her?"

Will got up and started to walk away. "Yeah, the swings are my favorite, but I've got to go. My mom wouldn't like me talking to you."

"I don't think she'd mind. I helped your mom get home last night, remember? Have you had dinner, yet?" Mick saw a younger version of himself in Will—resigned, but trying to be brave and muddle through. The boy obviously wasn't getting enough to eat. Maybe food was the path to take to win his trust.

"Not yet." Will looked up at him with a hopeful gleam in his eye. "Do you have any more takeout?"

"No, but maybe we could go get some." He held out his hand to the boy. "You should probably get your coat, though. It's cold out."

Will eyed his hand with some suspicion, but after giving Mick another once-over, he finally took it. "I don't mind the cold. It smells good."

"You can't smell cold," Mick said with a laugh. He closed his fingers around Will's small hand, a protective impulse washing over him.

"Yes, you can." Will nodded to emphasize his point. "It smells like crunchy leaves and dirt."

"Okay, I'll give you that one." They left Taunya's car behind and walked, turning the corner toward Adrienne's apartment. "If you don't want to wear your coat, maybe you could put on a long-sleeved shirt at least?"

"Yeah. I've got the one I wear to school. It has a soccer player on it, and it's my favorite." Will's face brightened and his steps seemed lighter. "I was goalie today at recess."

"That's awesome." Mick took in Will's upturned face; his smile and innocence took his breath away. That's how he'd been before he went to foster care. Full of hope, no matter what the situation at home had been like. When he looked at Will, all he could see was the "before" of his life. Foster care was the "after," and he was still dealing with the fallout from that. If Adrienne didn't come back soon, Will would need someone to shield him from any "afters" to keep that innocent determination intact. He could hardly take his eyes off the little boy by his side.

If only I'd had someone to step up for me, things might have been different. But he'd had no one.

They were nearly to the duplex when he heard sirens getting closer. He squeezed Will's hand, and they waited while two police cars and then Drew's sedan pulled up. Drew and Olivia got out, but Drew stayed behind while Olivia approached them with two officers trailing her. Mick inwardly groaned when he recognized one of them. Mont Morrill. He was a good officer, but he discussed all his calls with his wife, who was one of the biggest gossips in town.

Keep it cordial. "Hey," he said as Olivia approached.

"Where is she?" Olivia asked, sparing any niceties and spearing Mick with her gaze.

Mick took in the woman in front of him, her hair up, her business suit pressed and nearly perfect even after a day at work, her arms folded. She was probably giving him the look she gave suspects on the witness stand. "I have no idea." Mick kept his tone level, for Will's sake.

"If you helped her escape, you could be an accessory." Olivia slowly paced in front of him, her shoes making little clicking noises on the cement sidewalk. Did she expect him to crack under her careful eye?

"Do you honestly think I would help her steal my car?" Mick asked, his voice low and his eyebrows raised. "I came here hoping to find her before she could dump it."

Olivia gave him a measured look, then bent down to Will's level. "Is Hannah your mom's name?"

Fear skittered across his face and he shrank behind Mick. "Yes, but she told me never to call her that," he said, his voice small.

"It's okay, sweetheart. Do you know where your mom is? I just need to ask her some really important questions." Olivia's voice was soft and persuasive, a far cry from the tone she'd been throwing at Mick seconds before.

Will was silent, but didn't take his eyes off Olivia.

She stood and turned to Mont, who was hovering over her left shoulder. She dropped her voice a little, as if she didn't want Mick or Will to hear. But her words rang out like a sledgehammer to Mick's ears. "Have dispatch call CPS. We're going to need one of their investigators out here."

Will's hand trembled, and Mick held tighter, trying to calm the boy through his touch. "Wait. I'm in the process of becoming a licensed foster parent. Can't I just keep him with me?" He'd only decided to get his license a few weeks ago, but he'd been thinking about it for a long time.

"How far into the process are you?" Olivia's eyes narrowed, as if she were a human lie detector and her alarms were going off.

"I've just started taking the classes," Mick admitted. He knew from the look on her face that it wasn't enough. He should have started the process sooner.

"You're not authorized for a placement then," Olivia informed him, tapping her fingers on her sleeve and dismissing his words.

Mont took a step forward. "The on-call investigator isn't available. They want you to take him to emergency shelter care for tonight."

Mick shook his head before Mont had even finished speaking. No way did he want Will in a shelter. A seed of an idea formed, and before he could think it through, he blurted it out. "What if he were my son?"

Both officers, plus Drew and Olivia, seemed to freeze at his words. Even the wind stopped blowing, as if everyone was holding their breath. Olivia recovered first.

"Are you saying you're his father?" She sounded skeptical. "You didn't even know Hannah's real name."

"If I tell you he's mine," he said slowly, "You need to give us time to sort a few things out." He looked down at the boy. "He's been traumatized enough."

When Olivia didn't say no right away, hope rose in Mick. She looked down at Will for a long moment. "If you are claiming him, then we'll tell CPS that there's a relative present to take him. Mont, can you make sure dispatch gets that message?"

"Thank you." Mick stepped away, and Will was practically glued to his side. Even the mention of a shelter and Child Protective Services ran a chill down his spine. He didn't want that for Will, and it wouldn't happen if he could help it.

"Wait a minute. I have some more questions for you." Olivia was right on his heels as Mont talked into his radio. Mick held Will's hand even tighter as they moved closer to the corner where he'd left Taunya's car.

"Why don't I call you tomorrow and we can talk then?" Mick took a few more steps. He didn't want to look as if he was running, but he wanted to get Will out of there sooner rather than later. People were starting to gather on the sidewalk, gawking at the scene. This would definitely be a hot story around town. Not to mention that Mont's wife would make sure the embellished version reached every resident's ear by tomorrow. Would Mont say he'd claimed Will as his child? Would they believe it?

"Are we going for takeout now?" Will asked, just as they passed Drew standing near his own car.

Drew straightened and took a step toward them, as if he'd always been meant to be part of the conversation. "What a great idea! Why don't the four of us go get some food? I missed dinner and I'm starving. Then I can get to know this young man better while Olivia asks you her questions." Drew gave Mick a pointed look. "Win/win for everyone."

Will nodded, but looked up at Mick as if asking for permission. Panic was building inside Mick, but he'd made the claim, and he had to stick to it. For Will. "Okay, but we can't stay long. It's already getting late."

Olivia left the officers with some instructions, and they headed into Adrienne's apartment. Mick's feet were apparently rooted to the spot next to Drew's car. It took effort, but he got them moving again, keeping Will close as they moved away. "Okay, we'll meet you back at Rosie's."

Since it was the only restaurant in town, there weren't any other choices, but he didn't want to give Olivia or Drew a chance to suggest they should ride together. The sooner he could drive away, the easier it would be to gather his thoughts before Olivia grilled him for more information.

"We'll be right behind you," Olivia called. Her tone was challenging, as if she expected him not to show up, so they were going to give him an escort. But he wasn't the felon here. He only wanted to protect a little boy.

He kept Will's hand in his as they walked to Taunya's car. When they got there, Will looked disappointed. "You said you had a convertible and could ride with the top down when it wasn't snowing." His eyes were accusing.

"Your mom is, um, borrowing it right now." Mick opened the back door and helped Will get buckled in.

"You told that lady she stole it." Will shoved his hands in his pants pockets and turned his face away. "It's okay. Sometimes my mom steals things and tells me not to say anything. She probably did steal your car."

Mick took a deep breath, unsurprised at how observant the seven-year-old was of his mom's habits. "We all make mistakes sometimes."

Will shrugged, but didn't say anything, and Mick got into the driver's seat to head back to Rosie's. He knew exactly what Will was feeling, wanting to defend his mother and be proud of her, but knowing she did things that were wrong. That knowledge left him torn. Mick looked at the little boy in the rearview mirror. The pain of having a dysfunctional parent left so many scars. If Mick could take the confusion and heartache away from Will, he would, but Will would have to take that healing journey on his own. Even so, Mick wanted to be a support to him.

"When I was younger, my dad made some mistakes and stole things sometimes, too." He clenched the steering wheel tighter. He hadn't talked about his father to anyone in years. "But I promised myself I wouldn't be like him when I grew up."

"I've always wished for a dad. Are you . . . are you really my dad?" Will asked softly, meeting Mick's eyes in the rearview mirror. "That's what you told the lady."

Mick's breath caught. Lying wasn't a great example for a kid, either, but it hadn't been a mistake to imply Will was his. "No, I'm not your dad, but they wouldn't have let me take you home if I didn't say you were. I'm sorry."

"My mom told me my dad was a hero, and I just wondered . . ." His little voice trailed off. "I wish I knew him."

"I know what you mean. I don't have any memories of my mom," Mick confided. "I dreamed about her all the time and made up stories about her."

"I do that sometimes, too. Like I pretend that my dad is coming to get me, and we'll eat ice cream every day." Will looked out the window. "I wish it would come true."

"I do, too, buddy." They pulled into Rosie's parking lot, and Mick reached back to take hold of Will's hand. "But no matter what happens with your mom and dad, I want you to know I'll always be your friend, okay?"

"Okay." Will gave him a small smile.

Mick turned around and waited while Drew and Olivia parked beside them. They got out, and the four of them met at the sidewalk that led up to Rosie's. "You hungry, Will?" Olivia asked.

Will nodded, but didn't say anything. He slipped his hand into Mick's, and that tiny gesture added one more reason why Mick was taking a stand. Will needed him.

They all walked into the restaurant together and, thankfully, the dinner crowd had thinned. Not that they hadn't given everyone something to talk about the last time they were here, but Mick wanted to stay under the radar with this visit.

While they waited to be seated, Will pressed his nose against the display case, which held over a dozen different pies and cakes.

"I wish they had ice cream to look at," he said to Mick.

Olivia stood behind them and added in her two cents. "My favorite is mint chocolate brownie on a waffle cone. What's yours?"

"Waffle cones are for girls," Will announced. "I like moose tracks because I want to see a moose someday."

"I saw one once," Olivia offered, and Will's eyes got big. He was impressed. "It was when I was driving through Montana in a snowstorm, and the moose was running along the freeway. I was so surprised I had to swerve to get around it." She smiled at Will. "Maybe you and Mick could visit the zoo sometime to see one."

"That'd be fun." But Will didn't sound enthusiastic about that. Was he disappointed Mick wasn't his father? Hopefully he didn't let anything slip about that. This whole thing could be over before Olivia asked Mick a question. Remembering Will's little hand in his gave Mick an extra reassurance that he needed to go through with this little deception. *Not quite a lie,* Mick consoled himself, since he hadn't actually said straight out Will was his. He'd merely implied it.

Opting for seats at the counter with the old-fashioned stools, Mick ordered Will a grilled cheese sandwich and got a Turkey club for himself.

"Can you step over here for a moment?" Olivia asked Mick. She didn't waste any time, and seemed anxious to interrogate him. Was it a good thing she wanted to get him alone to question him? "Drew and Will can get better acquainted while we talk," she added, when he hesitated.

Mick's stomach twisted, but he agreed. What else could he do? He followed Olivia to the other side of the room and sat down in a booth, facing her.

"Tell me what you know about Hannah Dahlquist." She sounded stern, but the effect was ruined when she tucked a curl behind her ear. Mick took another good look at her. She'd taken her hair down. That's what had been different about her since they got to the restaurant. It was stunning, and the effect softened her somehow. Those caramel-colored curls framed her face, and Mick wanted to reach out to see if they were as silky as they looked. But he held still. The attorney part of Olivia was still there and they were playing a game that had high stakes for a little boy. Right now, though, she looked soft and approachable, no matter what tone her voice took. *She's still the same person who wants to put Will in foster care.*

He pulled his thoughts back to the issue at hand. "I've been helping her ever since I found out about Will." That was totally true. He'd been trying to convince her that Will needed a babysitter while she was at work when Olivia had barged into their conversation. He knew he had to keep his answers simple and with as much truth as possible. Olivia could probably spot a liar from twenty miles out.

"Did you have any idea there was a warrant out for her arrest?" Her hazel eyes were trained on him, and he could see she was the kind of lawyer who played hardball in the courtroom.

"Of course not. As you pointed out, she'd never even told me her real name." He folded his hands and rested them on the table, feeling a little like he was Olivia's witness. Well, he wouldn't fold.

"Did you know she sold drugs?" Olivia's face was impassive, but her eyes were penetrating, watching him for any signs of pretense or falsehood.

Mick shook his head. "No. I thought she had a problem with

alcohol. We were discussing childcare options when you walked up earlier."

Olivia seemed to relax a little bit at the mention of childcare. "When did you find out about Will?" Her voice was softer when she said Will's name. Mick decided he liked her tone better that way.

He glanced over at Drew and Will, who were laughing together. He couldn't say he'd first seen Will last night. "It feels like we just met, but at the same time, like I've known him forever." Corny, but the truth. He'd never had such a fierce reaction to protect a child.

Olivia was watching him, silently evaluating his answer, when she leaned forward, her eyes full of compassion. "I met him a few months ago. I really thought I could help him, but by the time CPS showed up at their Salt Lake apartment, Hannah had disappeared and taken Will with her." Olivia shook her head. "It's hard to see kids get caught up in the messes their parents make, and I've been kicking myself for not acting sooner."

"So you were going to put him in foster care and call it good? You're sad you didn't get him in the system sooner?" Mick folded his arms, any favorable feelings for her evaporating. He tried to push down his frustration and stay passive, knowing that would help his case more than anything else. "Sometimes having the government step in isn't the best option."

"At least he'd have a stable home." She narrowed her eyes and tilted her head, trying to read his thoughts. "It doesn't matter now if he has you, right?"

Mick didn't even hesitate. "That's right." He motioned to the counter, where the waitress had just served Will his food. "Guess we better go eat. I need to get Will home and settled."

"If Hannah contacts you or Will, call the police immediately." Olivia slid out of her seat and stood next to him, the top of her head just brushing his chin. "I know it's hard, but we really need to take her off the streets. Hannah's running with some dangerous people, and the sooner we cut off the arms of the organization, the safer we'll all be."

"She's that deeply involved?" Mick shook his head, surprise mixed with anger running through him. Hannah had put her own needs ahead of her child, and Will would be the one to suffer for it. "I honestly wouldn't have guessed it." He thought back to last night and wished he'd pressed her more about Will and his care, made her see what she was doing. But who was he kidding? His own father had been an addict just like her, and nothing had ever made him see beyond his own needs.

Olivia was studying him now, her eyes watchful. He turned away, not wanting her seeing any emotion on his face.

"She got trapped like so many others. The dealer got her hooked on drugs, then forced her to deal to get her next fix." Olivia eyed him, as if she were reading his thoughts. "You had no idea at all?"

"We mostly talked about Will." Also true, since he'd only had two interactions with Hannah beyond her serving his food as a waitress, and she could barely remember the first one through a drunken haze. He still had so many more questions about Hannah, and no one to get the answers from. He certainly couldn't ask Olivia. Claiming Will meant he should know a lot more about his mother than he really did, so asking personal questions would give him away. "Don't worry. If she comes back, I'll definitely call the police."

Olivia followed his gaze over to Will. "You know I'll be checking into things, and though I'm letting Will go with you for the moment, if anything happens to him, I'll hold you personally responsible. That said, as a father, you may want to think about counseling. He's had to grow up with circumstances no child should have to deal with."

"I agree. You don't have to worry, I'll take care of him." He walked over and stood beside Will, settling his hand on his shoulder. "How's the grilled cheese?"

Will looked up at him, a string of cheese hanging from his mouth to the bread. "It's great."

Mick smiled. "Looks like it. Should we get a takeout bag and head home? It's been a crazy day."

"Sure." Will didn't argue or seem upset. He got off the stool while Mick asked for a to-go box. Emma, one of the youngest waitresses, slowly got the box out. With the way she kept looking from Olivia to Mick, it was easy to see she had questions about what was really going on. She was a former student, and Mick had no doubt Emma's best friend AnnaLise would be the first one she texted on her break to give her the scoop. The rumor mill turned quickly in Lincoln, and while Mick had been the subject of some gossip before, he wished he could insulate Will. Hopefully it would die down sooner rather than later.

Emma didn't take long to pack up their sandwiches, thankfully, since it was awkward standing next to Olivia and Drew without anything to say. Olivia was still watching him closely, which made him antsy. He let out a breath and tried to unobtrusively relieve some tension. She was good. The woman could probably make the most hardened criminals feel nervous.

"It was nice to meet you, Will," Drew told the boy. "I never knew there were thirty-two panels on a soccer ball. You're a smart kid."

"Thanks." Will watched the takeout bag in Mick's hand as if he was afraid it would disappear. Mick needed to get the boy somewhere that he could eat in peace.

"See you later," Mick said, as he ushered Will toward the door, glad to finally be able to leave.

"We'll talk again soon," Olivia told Mick before he got far. "I'd like to keep in touch." She gave him a pointed look, and he knew she meant to check on whether Hannah ever contacted him. Since he'd only met her yesterday, he was pretty sure a phone call or visit was a slim possibility. But having *Olivia* stay in contact wouldn't be unwelcome. When she wasn't being a lawyer and making him nervous, she was someone he could see himself wanting to know better.

If nothing else, he wanted to stay on her good side. "You know where to find me," he said and gave her a smile.

They finally made it to the parking lot, when he remembered he didn't have a car. He couldn't borrow Taunya's again, since her shift wouldn't be over until closing time, and she'd need it. He sighed, debating whether to go back inside and ask for a ride or start walking. His house wasn't far, but he had a child with him and it was getting cold.

"Are we really going to your house?" Will raised his eyes to Mick's. He could see the uncertainty and had an overwhelming urge to reassure Will that he'd be taken care of from this point forward—if Mick had anything to do with it.

"We've got to finish our dinner, don't we?" He put his arm around the boy's shoulders. "And we should probably have a talk about what comes next."

"And about my mom?" Will asked with a resigned tone.

"Yeah," Mick told him, as they started walking down the sidewalk toward home. "We've got some things to sort out."

Which was the understatement of the year.

CHAPTER FOUR

Olivia slowly walked back to the counter and sat down on the stool next to Drew. Part of her wanted to go after Mick and question him further, but she needed more information first, so she stayed where she was. Swiveling around, she faced her brother. "Do you think Will is his kid?" She still hadn't quite gotten over the shock of that little revelation.

"I'm not sure. Either way, the whole town will be talking about it by Monday morning." Drew didn't seem perturbed by the discovery, as he picked up a pickle spear. "You know how it is in Lincoln. News like that will travel fast."

Olivia snitched a fry off his plate for herself and took a bite. Glancing around, she noticed only a few patrons were still there after the dinner rush, but she leaned closer to Drew just in case anyone tried to listen in. She was done providing the gossips with new material today. "Something feels off about this whole thing."

"Like what?" Drew tilted his head while he finished chewing his bite of pickle. "Is it really surprising that someone like Mick would have a child he didn't know about? He's been a player for as long as I've known him."

She shook her head, that description not sitting right with her. "He's a serial dater, but I've never heard you say anything about him toying with a woman's feelings or cheating on a girlfriend."

Drew looked thoughtful. "Okay, you're right. He just doesn't date women more than a few times, from what I can tell. To me, that's a player, a guy who dates around with no thought of ever settling down or making a commitment."

Olivia shook her head. "And to me, a player is a guy who doesn't care about a woman's feelings and is in it for whatever he can get out of that woman or out of the next woman to come along."

She thought back to her own experience with David, someone who hadn't even given her a full five minutes of his attention before he was flirting with someone else. From what little she'd seen and heard about Mick, he wasn't like that. "There's definitely a difference."

"I suppose." Drew finished up his meal. "I haven't given it a lot of thought before. It doesn't matter, though. If Mick is the dad, his life is forever changed."

"I don't know what to think yet. At first, Mick acted like he wanted to keep Will as a foster child, but then he claimed to be the biological father. He seemed unsure, though. On the other hand, that uneasiness would make sense if he'd just found out Will was his, and he was trying to keep the matter quiet. But there seemed more to it somehow." Olivia leaned on the counter, her chin in her hand. "I just can't imagine him with Hannah Dahlquist, but his attachment to Will is obvious."

When Mick and Will had left the restaurant, he'd put his arm around the boy, and, for all appearances, they'd seemed close. Even with that evidence, though, Olivia couldn't explain her gut reaction that something wasn't right. She just knew it.

Drew was watching her as if she was one of his students reciting Shakespeare for the first time. "I don't know what to think about Will, really, or what he means to Mick. It's hard to read the man since he keeps his feelings to himself." Drew wiped his fingers on a napkin. "Do you want to come back to the house? Tori and Cal would love to see you."

"Rain check? I've got to get back to the office." Olivia twisted around to get off the stool.

Drew put his hand on her arm and leaned down to meet her eyes. "You work too much. If you're going back to the office because of Mick, it can wait until Monday morning."

"I have to update Hannah's file and fill out a report on what happened tonight. It won't take long, so don't worry, big brother." She stood next to him and looked into his concerned face. "I can take care of myself."

"It's my job to worry." He pulled her in for a hug. "I only want what's best for you."

"I know." She gave him an extra squeeze before she pulled back. "I promise I'll do something fun this weekend."

He raised his eyebrows just enough to give her a skeptical look. "I'm going to hold you to that. And your idea of fun better not have anything to do with reading offense reports, preparing motions, or Mick."

"You're worse than Mom," Olivia said with a laugh. But they knew her well. "Well, thanks for a surprising evening."

"Nothing's ever dull when you're around." Drew paid the bill, and they walked out together so he could drive her back to the high school. Olivia's car was the only one left in the parking lot. Drew pulled up beside it, but before she could get out, he nudged her shoulder. "Come visit anytime. I'm always available for you."

"I will. Thanks again." Olivia waved and got into her car, anxious to get back to the office to puzzle out what wasn't adding up with Mick Donovan and his story. Her mind had been going through the little she'd been able to glean, searching for answers that made sense, but kept coming up short. The problem would continue to swirl around in her head, which was why she had to go back to the office. She'd never sleep tonight if she didn't.

Getting on the freeway, she thought back to the few times she'd interacted with Mick before today. As a chaperone at the school dances, he'd always seemed professional, but smooth and charming to her and a few of his female colleagues. He'd even tried to make the leap from the friend zone with Tori before she'd admitted to her feelings for Drew. When it came down to it, though, Mick had stepped aside without a lot of fuss, and Olivia had been impressed by that. He definitely drew people to him easily. Tonight, the look in his eyes had held vulnerability, as if he silently needed her to understand something he couldn't put into words. But what?

Of course that look could be explained if he'd truly just found out Will was his child. Yet, Olivia had read Hannah's file a million times. It mostly detailed her arrests and convictions.

Olivia didn't remember any details about Will's father. Had Hannah ever mentioned him? Could the world really be so small that he would be Mick?

When she finally got to the dark and deserted office building, she locked her car and went inside. Being at the office after hours had never been creepy for her since she'd practically lived here the first year after she'd been hired. She knew every nook and cranny of this place. And tonight she needed answers more than she needed sleep.

Going through the reception area, she pulled out her badge to unlock the door. She didn't bother to turn on any lights, the glow from the security lamps just enough for her to see where she was going. The shadows from the desks, computers, and file folders were familiar and comfortable, like old friends welcoming her home.

She bypassed the conference room and Jana's desk, heading for her office. When this particular space had come open, her boss, Sam Wood, had offered it to her. She'd said yes immediately. Since it was at the end of a long hall, she had some of the benefits of having a corner office, only without the great view. Olivia also loved the modicum of privacy, since no one could just walk by. If they were going down to the end of the hallway, they were probably coming to see her.

She made it there in record time and strode to her desk, still covered in files. Kicking off her shoes, she sat down and turned on her computer and with a few clicks to her shortcuts for client files, Hannah's came up on the screen. It wasn't hard to find the information that should have given her the name of Will's father, but she came up empty. All she had was a birth certificate that didn't list a father's name. Olivia sat back, staring at the birth records, willing the father's name to appear —but the line stayed blank. Where could she look next for the link between Hannah and Mick?

On a hunch, she searched through vital records for Mick's name. His DMV record, as well as his property records, came up right away. He didn't have any speeding tickets, and he owned a nice piece of land in Lincoln. Idly wondering why a shop teacher needed a two-acre lot, she scrolled through his life in the public records. Telling herself she wasn't a stalker, and all this was necessary to close a case, she made sure to verify every record, from his background check done for his teaching certificate, to his utility bills. He looked good from every angle.

But just as Olivia was about to go back over Hannah's records with a fine-toothed comb, she noticed Mick's name pop up as a witness on a criminal case when he was a minor. She looked at it, her heart rate increasing. A sense of foreboding washed over her, as if the universe was warning her that by clicking that icon, the answers she needed would appear and they wouldn't be pretty. She hesitated, her finger hovering over the mouse.

Quickly clicking on it before she could change her mind, she watched the document come up. It didn't take long to read the first few pages. Mick had been interviewed by a judge when his foster parents had been put on trial for abuse and neglect.

Shutting her emotions in a dark corner of her mind so she could be objective, she read about his mother dying when he was a baby, and how his father had been arrested and put in jail on drug charges. Mick entered foster care at six years old and was placed with numerous families over the next seven years. But when she saw the name of the last family he'd been placed with, she closed the file. Hawkins. She didn't need to read anymore. The Hawkins' case had been headline news back in the day for the horrific abuse all of the foster kids suffered in that home. Knowing now that Mick was one of them made her stomach turn, but it also gave her some insight into the man Mick had become.

Olivia sat back in her chair and closed her eyes, trying to push down her emotions again. If even a tenth of what the papers had reported about the Hawkins case was true, he'd suffered horribly. No wonder he hadn't wanted DCFS called in on Will's case. There was no way he'd trust the system after going through abuse like that. No matter how she assured him that there were new checks and balances in place since he'd been in foster care, those scars would run deep, and she doubted he would take her word for it. Even with all those safeguards in place, the system wasn't perfect, so his fear might be justified in a small way.

With a sigh, she looked over Mick's file one more time, looking for the connection to Hannah. Maybe they'd met in foster care. But when Olivia went back to Hannah's file and read it over again, one part of a statement to a judge before sentencing stood out.

"My daughter Hannah is a first-time offender. She only turned to drugs to dull the pain after the father of her child was killed in action in Afghanistan."

A tiny part of her heart squeezed with compassion at the mother's plea for her daughter, but the information that jumped out at her was that Will's father had been killed in Afghanistan, even though he wasn't named. Had Hannah ever told anyone who he was? She looked down at the statement again. Was there even a remote chance . . .? With one more look at Mick's records, she confirmed he had served in the military, but not in the same time frame of the mother's statement. Olivia had her answer about Mick's claim. He wasn't Will's father.

And yet . . . she went over the words Mick had specifically used. *If he were my son . . . If he's mine . . .* The way he'd claimed Will had been ambiguous, as if he was giving Olivia an out so she wouldn't be held accountable if there were consequences for taking Will. But was there a bigger issue here? With his history in the foster care system, why would he want to become a foster parent? What was his true connection to Will? So many questions.

And Olivia was determined to get the answers.

CHAPTER FIVE

Mick watched Will finish off his dinner as if it were the last food on the planet. Every now and then he glanced up at Mick before he bent to take a bite.

"Did you get full?" Mick finally asked when it looked like Will was done.

"Yeah." Will wiped his mouth on the back of his hand and looked around the room as if it were the first time he'd seen it. "Where am I going to sleep?"

Mick stood and started to gather up the plasticware. "I have a guest bedroom that you can use." But as he spoke, he realized he didn't have any clothes for Will. That was a problem. He leaned his hip against the cupboard. "Hey, we left your house so quickly, we didn't get to pack a suitcase or anything." And of course, he didn't have a car at the moment to go get any. Walking home from Rosie's with Will had definitely moved getting a rental car to the top of his list.

Will didn't seem concerned about wearing the same clothes. "That's okay. I'll just sleep in what I have on."

That didn't necessarily sound bad, but in the interest of being a responsible adult, Mick mentally went through his wardrobe. "Maybe I can scrounge up something for you to wear for pajamas at least." He threw the trash away and started down the hall. "Let me go look."

Mick walked into the guest bedroom with Will on his heels. He opened up the closet where he'd stored some of the clothes he'd planned to take to Goodwill. Pulling out the box, he started to empty out the clothes in it. T-shirts, sweats, shorts, pants, and some ties that were still in good condition. He separated a t-shirt and some sweats with an elastic waistband. "Maybe these will do for tonight." He held the shirt up for Will's approval.

Will slowly read the words written across the front, sounding them out. "*Saw-dust? You mean man glit-ter.*" He laughed and said it again. "Man glitter."

Mick laughed along with him. "Yep, sawdust is manly." He turned and pulled a wooden treasure box off the dresser. "When I made this a few years ago, there was a ton of sawdust." It was a basic box, but he'd spent a lot of time meticulously carving geometric designs on the sides. A labor of love that had turned out to be one of his favorites. He flipped the lid open to show the inside.

"You made that?" Will looked impressed, even though the box had been empty.

"In the daytime I teach kids at the high school how to work with wood, and in the evenings, I have a space out back where I make furniture and custom orders." He set the treasure box on the dresser. "You want to see my workshop?"

"Sure." Will followed him out of the room, staying close behind. "You must like wood a lot."

"Yeah." Mick walked through the house and out across the lawn toward the shop. They crunched over the layer of leaves in the yard and Mick made a mental reminder to get the rake out tomorrow. "I like taking a piece of wood and transforming it into something beautiful." He unlocked the shop door and stepped inside, turning on the lights.

The room was a little larger than a two-car garage, with a nook for a worktable and space for all his tools, which is what drew him to it in the first place. The rest of the shop was taken up by his works-in-progress.

"Wow." Will's eyes were immediately drawn to the table in the middle of the room. "What's that?"

"A totem pole. A lady ordered it because she loves everything about the people in the Native American Northwest and so she asked me to make a replica for her." He ran his hands over the top of the piece. Each section had had its own challenges, but he was proud of how it had turned out. He'd be packaging this one up in the next day or two to send off.

"So people just ask you to make things for them?" Will walked over and stood in front of the totem pole to look up at the winged creature at the top.

"Yep. It's a nice side job for me." He moved to the far end of the room where the rocking chair sat. "I'm almost done with this one, too." He ran his hand over the carvings on the back of the chair. It hadn't been a hard piece, but he was especially proud of the flowers carved along the back.

"Can I sit in it?" Will asked, standing next to Mick. As they both looked down at the chair, Mick noticed the boy copying his stance. His heart melted a little at the sight.

"Sure." He stepped away so Will could sit down. "See how it feels."

Will settled into the chair and rocked back and forth, a smile lighting his face. "It works."

"Did you think it wouldn't?" Mick chuckled at the boy's obvious surprise.

Concentrating on the rocking motion, Will shrugged and rocked harder. "I don't know."

An honest answer. Mick walked over to his worktable and sat down, picking up the owl he'd been working on. "Now this one has been harder than some of those others." He tilted the owl toward Will. "Carving feathers isn't easy at all. Not if you want them to look realistic."

Will stopped rocking and came to stand beside him, blowing on the sawdust left from last night's work. He laughed as it floated to the ground. "It looks good to me."

Mick smiled at the boy. "Thanks." He blew on the owl, too, and more sawdust coated them.

"Man glitter," Will said, with a grin.

"Right." Mick tousled the little boy's hair. "And we better shake it off before we track little trails of dust through the house. It's almost time for bed."

They shook themselves like a dog would after a bath and laughed the whole time. Will leaned closer until his head was nearly touching Mick's forearm. He just stood there for a moment, before he swallowed loudly and clenched his hands together. "Do you know when my mom is coming back?"

Mick put his arm around Will's shoulders. "I'm not sure. Has she ever left you before?"

"She always comes back." Will looked up at Mick with a pleading look on his face. "I like it here with you. Can I stay until she comes to get me?" he asked softly.

Mick's insides churned. If the alternative was foster care, he wanted to say yes immediately. But he knew that Will might not be able to stay, especially if Olivia dug very far into the situation. And from what he knew of her, that was a distinct probability. "I'm not sure. I hope so."

Will's knuckles were white as he pressed his hands together, but he nodded and turned away, as if used to disappointment. Mick's heart squeezed, but he had to be truthful with the boy. Trusting adults was harder for kids whose parents weren't reliable. He would earn Will's trust by always being honest and keep that as a foundation between them if he could.

Will didn't say anything on their way back to the house, and Mick didn't force the issue. The boy had had a long day, and it was probably better if they had a good night's sleep and some time to process. Mick looked down at Will, just as he yawned, confirming his thoughts. "Hey, do you remember the way to your room?"

"Yes." He looked up at Mick. "Can I stay here all day tomorrow, at least?"

"You bet." Mick put his arm around the boy. "Maybe we can go to the park and kick the ball around for a while. Saturdays are play days, right?"

"They are?" Will's eyes lit up. "I love going to the park. Do you have a ball?"

"I sure do." Mick wanted to hug him. How could a child not

know that weekends were for playing? For a moment he wanted to ask what Will had usually done on Saturdays with his mother, but held that question in check.

"Can we go as soon as we wake up?" Will stepped away and moved toward the hall. "I can wake up early so we can get a lot of kicks in."

"Whoa, whoa," Mick said, lengthening his stride to catch him. "We can't go too early because the sun won't be up, and it will be cold." Will's face fell a bit, so Mick rushed on. "But, how about let's wake up, eat some pancakes with butter and syrup, maybe clean the house a bit, and then go. The sun is sure to be up by then."

"Okay." The boy's smile came back as he headed for his room. "See you tomorrow."

"Hey, haven't you forgotten something?" Mick tilted his head and raised his eyebrows.

Will frowned and a little crease appeared in his forehead, as if he was thinking hard of anything he could have forgotten. "Like what?"

"After the man glitter and everything we ate tonight, you better wash your face and brush your teeth, right?" Mick pointed toward the bathroom. "The washcloths are in the cupboard next to the sink, and there's a new toothbrush in the drawer that you can have. Do you need help with any of that?"

Will's frown turned to a grin before he shook his head. "No, I can do that myself. Well, except for opening the toothpaste."

Mick followed him into the bathroom and got the toothbrush out of the package and opened the toothpaste. "If you need anything in the night, my room is right there at the end of the hall, okay? 'Night."

"Thanks, Mick," Will said softly as he shut the door.

Mick nodded and went into the living room. He sat down and picked up the TV remote. Changing channels until he found a football game on, he leaned back to get comfortable. He could hear the water running and obvious sounds of Will getting ready for bed. It was comforting somehow and Mick felt like he'd done a good thing. Will wasn't in an emergency shelter or a foster home tonight. He was safe here with Mick. That's what mattered.

But even with that thought, he knew he wasn't totally prepared to have a child. What was he going to do for after-school childcare for Will? And if something happened, like a medical emergency, Mick didn't have any legal guardianship or claim to him. He'd have no way of signing for medical care or putting him on Mick's insurance plan. If, by some miracle, Mick was allowed to keep Will, there would definitely be a lot of issues to work out.

Once Will was done in the bathroom and had gone to bed, Mick didn't have to wait long before all was quiet down the hall. Rubbing his shoulders, Mick turned off the TV and headed for his own room. Opening Will's door a crack, he peeked in. The boy was curled into a ball on one side of the bed, his covers making a cocoon around him. His face was peaceful and innocent.

Mick backed away from the scene in front of him, a ball of emotion making a lump in his throat. Would Will have had that same look if he'd been in a shelter or anywhere else? There was no way to be sure, but in Mick's mind, this was the best option —to have Will here.

Mick got ready for bed, and when he finally slept, the old

nightmare came back. The one that haunted him most. He was in the punishment closet. His stomach twisted in knots as he tried to see through the darkness. Deal with the pain from the whipping he'd taken. But most of all, being hungry.

So hungry.

He didn't make a sound, knowing that would only bring another beating. But he cried silently, feeling tears slip down his cheeks. If only he could behave. Be a good boy. Then none of this would happen.

But the familiar dream changed. He wasn't alone. Someone was next to him in the closet and they were crying, too. Mick lifted his head off his knees, wanting to see who it was. When he looked over, he recoiled. Will's face stared back at him. Mick pounded on the door. He didn't care if he got a beating. Will couldn't be here!

Mick woke up in a cold sweat, disoriented. It was still dark outside, and he immediately flipped on the lamp and let the light flood his room. Flopping back on the bed, he tried to slow his breathing. He wasn't a kid anymore. No one would hurt him like that again, and Will was fine in the next room.

He punched his pillow a few times and tried to get comfortable. He wouldn't let his memories or the uncertainty of his situation with Will get the best of him. He tried to put the images out of his mind, working on his breathing exercises to relax and imagining his peaceful cabin by the lake. But after an hour, none of his coping mechanisms were working. He finally gave up and looked at the clock. It was five in the morning, so not crazy early. He could get up and work on his owl carving. Or maybe he'd get up and make Will a nice breakfast. Anything was better than lying in bed, reliving a part of his life he wanted to forget.

Trying to be as quiet as possible, Mick decided to go with bacon, eggs, *and* pancakes. Before long the whole house smelled like bacon, and Will appeared in the kitchen just as Mick finished up the first batch.

"Morning," he said to the boy. "I've got pancakes and eggs and bacon if you're hungry."

Will's eyes got round. "All that for breakfast?"

"I was thinking, if we're going to be running and kicking the ball at the park, we've got to keep our energy up. We need lots of protein and carbs so we have something to burn." Mick finished dishing up Will's plate and set it down in front of him.

He dug right in, going for the pancakes first. Mick dished himself a plate and sat across from Will. "Did you sleep okay?"

Will nodded, but his focus was on his food. He'd done the same thing yesterday, blocking out almost everything else when there was food nearby. That reaction alone said he'd gone hungry more than once in his short life. Anger toward Hannah flared, but Mick tamped his emotions down. It wouldn't do any good to be mad at an addict. The best thing he could do right now was take care of Will.

The two of them ate in silence, but once he was done, Will looked over at him. "When can we leave for the park?"

"Well, we need to clean up the kitchen first." Mick glanced out the window. The sun was trying valiantly to shine through the clouds. "We'll probably have to dress warm."

Will's face fell. "I didn't want to tell you before, but I don't have a coat."

Pity and sadness meshed together in Mick, but he kept his

face carefully neutral. "That's okay. We'll stop by the Blue Bee on our way and get you one."

"My mom used to look in the windows of the Blue Bee. They have lots of clothes there that she liked, but we always had to go to Value Village." He bit his lip. "Do you think my mom's coming back today?"

"I don't know, buddy." Mick reached out to put his hand on the boy's shoulder. "But we can still have some fun together while we wait and see, okay?"

Will agreed, but kept his face averted. Mick saw a tear roll down his cheek.

Wanting to distract him, Mick stood quickly and carried his plate to the sink. "How are you at drying dishes?"

"I don't know." Will shrugged. "I've never tried it."

Within minutes, Mick had him drying dishes like a pro. They laughed and talked about all the trick moves they were going to do at the park, each story getting bigger and crazier.

"We're going to have to stop at Jake's before we go to the park, so I can get another car," Mick said, not wanting to kill the good mood, but wanting to let Will know what to expect.

"Because my mom took your car?" Will's demeanor went from relaxed to alert in the blink of an eye. "Are you mad at her?"

"No, I'm not mad. But I need to rent a car so we don't have to walk everywhere." He smiled and headed toward the front door. He'd put on his warmest sweatshirt this morning and found a smaller one for Will. "Maybe Jake will have another convertible."

"Could we drive with the top down?" Will's eyes brightened again as he moved next to Mick. The boy was hardly two steps away from his side, which testified to his need to feel secure. "I've never done that."

"Sure, but you might get cold." Mick grabbed the sweatshirt he'd found for Will and watched him put it on. The sleeves went over his hands by about six inches, so Mick knelt and rolled them up. "Maybe this will help until we can get you a new coat."

Will pointed to the picture of the Lincoln Lions High School logo on the front. "And we match."

"We're both Lincoln Lion fans today." Mick locked the front door, then held out his hand before they started down the street. It was about six blocks to Main Street, but luckily, Jake's Used Car Lot and Rental was on the side closest to them. Mick watched Will carefully, making sure he wasn't shivering, but he seemed fine. They talked nearly non-stop about a boy in his class that also loved soccer, but made up his own rules when they played. The group that played soccer at recess was apparently accepting of Will and that reassured Mick. He was sure Will went to school without bathing regularly, possibly in the same clothes, but it didn't sound like he'd been bullied. The way Will talked, even though his home life had been chaotic, he had a relatively normal life at school. That could be a stabilizing factor as his living situation was sorted out. At least, Mick hoped it would.

They made it to Jake's and went inside. It had a small office, with a counter and a cash register at the front, and a desk beyond it, but the best thing about it right now was how warm it was. Mick drew Will to his side while they waited for Jake. They didn't have to wait long. Jake came in from the back with a little girl next to him. They both wore a smile as they walked toward them. Well, with Jake's bushy beard, it was actually a little hard to tell if it was a smile, but Mick thought the corners of his mouth were definitely tilted up underneath.

"Haven't seen you in a while." Jake held out his hand and Mick shook it. "What can I do for you?"

"I need to rent a car for a while." Mick glanced out the window at the available rentals. "I'm hoping you have something a little sporty."

Jake laughed. "Sorry. All I've got are four-door sedans right now. They're the most popular with dependable reputations and good gas mileage."

Mick looked down at Will, whose disappointed expression was nearly comical. "I guess I'll have to take one of those then. If you're sure you don't have anything else."

"Sorry." Jake pulled out a clipboard of paper. "Let's get you started."

Will wandered over to the window to look at the cars, and Jake found a TV remote. He turned on a cartoon for the kids and the noise drew Will to a bench to watch. The little girl ignored the cartoon and focused on Will.

"My name's Charly," she said. He merely nodded and didn't even blink when she sat beside him.

Jake looked at the two kids and back at the TV. "Remember when there used to be Saturday morning cartoons? I got up early for those every weekend when I was a kid. Now it's twenty-four hour cartoons, and it's not as special."

"Me, too. The good old days." Mick grabbed a pen from the cup at his elbow and started filling out the paperwork. Jake watched for a minute and Mick could feel that he wanted to say something, but was hesitating.

"I'm not one to gossip, you know that," Jake finally said. "But as a man who's a single father myself, I know how hard it can be. If you ever need any help, I'm around."

Mick held in his surprise. He didn't know Jake very well, but their few interactions had been talking about cars. And here he was offering his help to someone he thought was a fellow single father. "Thanks, man," he said. "We're just sorting a few things out."

"Well, the offer stands." He turned to pick up some keys. "I've got a nice blue sedan out there with a few bells and whistles that might make up for not being a sports car."

Mick chuckled. "Thanks, I appreciate that. And your offer." He finished up the paperwork as quickly as he could, and before the cartoon had finished, they were saying goodbye to Jake and Charly. Climbing into the blue rental car, Will was fascinated with the backup camera screen and the moon roof.

"This isn't so bad," Will finally said. "Even if it isn't a convertible."

"I think so, too." Mick pulled up at the Blue Bee and turned around with a smile. "Now let's go get you a new coat."

They looked both ways and crossed the street to the clothing store. The children's section was conveniently positioned in the front and Will started looking through the racks of coats and snow pants. The owner of the shop, Beatrice Watts, was behind the counter and glanced up at them over her glasses. "You boys need any help?"

"We're looking for a coat," Mick told her, glancing back at Will. He was eyeing a black one that had a large red stripe across the back.

Beatrice got up and slowly made her way over to them. Her

white hair was done up in a small beehive hairdo from the 60s and Mick briefly wondered how old she was. He'd never dare ask, though. Beatrice, or Bea as everyone called her, didn't put up with any *shenanigans*, as she called it.

She made it over to them and looked at the coat Will had obviously chosen. "That one has some newfangled insulation in it that supposedly keeps you really warm. And the hood is detachable."

Will looked up at Mick. He desperately wanted that coat, but he wasn't going to ask for it. When Mick had been young, he'd wanted a pair of shoes that lit up whenever you walked, but he'd never dared ask, either. Well, today, Will didn't need to ask.

"We'll take it." Mick took the coat off the display hanger. "But maybe we should try it on first to see if we got the right size."

The excitement in Will's eyes was heartwarming. He slipped the coat on. "It fits!"

"That's a perfect fit if I ever did see one," Bea put in. She reached down and pulled off the price tag. "I'll just ring this up and you won't have to take it off."

She shuffled back to the cash register with Mick and Will following behind her. "Janice dropped in last night for a visit," she said casually, as she poked the keys on the register.

Mick's heart sank. Janice was Mont's wife, and there weren't too many reasons she'd make a special trip to the Blue Bee, except to share the newest gossip. "Oh yeah?" he said noncommittally.

Bea glanced at Will. "For what it's worth, I'm glad you

claimed the boy. You two make a fine pair." She smiled as Mick handed over his debit card. "Glad you did right by him."

Even though Bea didn't know the details, her words still gave Mick a warm feeling. With Jake and Bea being so accepting, maybe the people in this town weren't as judgmental as he'd thought.

"Thanks, Bea," he said as he took his debit card and the receipt.

"You two stay warm," she called after them as they left the shop. "It's going to snow later on today."

Will waved back at her before he slipped his hand into Mick's. Once he got Will buckled in the back seat, Mick got in and started the car. "Who wants to head to the park?" Mick asked as they pulled away from the curb.

"Me!" Will's face was wreathed in smiles, and every time Mick glanced at him in the rearview mirror, he was stroking the outside of his coat. "Wait until Adam sees my new coat," he finally said. "It's so warm and has a red stripe. That's my favorite color."

"Just what every soccer player needs." Mick pulled into the park near the center of town, which had a playground and a nice-sized soccer field. He picked up the ball from the floor of the car. "You ready?"

"Ready." Will unbuckled and climbed out of the car. They went over to the field, and Mick wasn't surprised when Will showed him all the tricks he'd mastered with the ball. His best one was balancing the ball on his forehead. He could keep it there for thirty-three seconds. When Mick tried it, his best time was only twenty, which Will did not let him forget.

After they'd played for a couple of hours, they headed back

to the car, laughing and talking about how Mick could improve his head balancing skills. It had been such a fun day, but when he saw Olivia parked next to them, wearing a serious look on her face, his stomach sank. That could only mean one thing.

And it wasn't good.

CHAPTER SIX

Olivia watched them approach her, the joy they'd had in the park nowhere to be seen. Mick's shoulders were tense, and he wasn't smiling. She'd seen that a lot in courtroom opponents when they knew she'd found a discrepancy of some sort. Mick had to know his deception couldn't last. Hopefully he'd listen to what she had to say and understand what had to be done.

Will seemed to sense the change in Mick, and his brow furrowed with anxiety. Olivia wished she had good news, the kind that would put smiles back on their faces. The only words that would accomplish that, though, would be to say he could stay with Mick. And it was the one thing she couldn't allow.

"Hey," she said when they got close enough to hear her. "Looks like you were having some fun out there."

Mick stopped and shifted the ball to his other hand. "We were. How did you find us?"

Well, he certainly got straight to the point. "In a town this small, it's not hard to find people. Especially when I know how much one of you loves soccer." She focused on Will. "Looked like you were teaching Mick a few things out there."

"I was showing him how to balance a ball . . . on his head," Will said, his voice wavering as he looked between the two of them.

Mick moved around to the side of the car. "Hey, buddy, why don't you get in while I talk to Ms. Dalton for a minute."

Will didn't protest, just took the ball and got in the backseat. Mick shut the door and then walked over to face her. "Did you find Hannah? Or my car?"

Olivia shoved her hands in her pockets. It was getting colder, feeling more and more like winter was right around the corner. Looking at the stony expression of the man in front of her chilled her even more. With his mouth set in a hard line, and his eyes like blue granite staring a hole through her, he was as cold as the air around them.

"No updates on that. Since we both know you're not his father, I went ahead and called Child Protective Services." Olivia glanced toward the car where Will sat. She was grateful the door was shut and he couldn't hear. Breaking the news to him shouldn't be done in a parking lot. "He's been assigned a caseworker and a new placement. I don't like being lied to."

Mick dropped his gaze. Sucking in a breath, he pressed his hands together to blow on them. "Listen, can we go back to my place and talk about this? I'd like to get Will out of the cold."

"Okay." Letting him explain would be good for all of them. She wanted to understand his side, and they both needed to talk about what was going to happen to Will. At least being on Mick's home turf might encourage him to discuss everything and soften the blow of Will's having to leave. Watching how they'd played together and laughed so often made her heart twist with sympathy. The bond they'd formed was even stronger now.

They all climbed in their cars and headed to Mick's house. Olivia turned up the heater full blast and put her fingers as close to the vents as she could, but they stayed cold. Having ice-cold hands was a weird thing that happened to her when she got anxious. But having that reaction to a case of nerves was better than some of the alternatives she'd seen, especially when a janitor had to be called to clean up the mess.

Mick pulled into his driveway with Olivia right behind him. When they got out, Will stayed next to Mick, barely giving Olivia more than a glance.

They all walked into the living room, and Will took off his coat. "Let me hang that up for you, buddy," Mick offered, before he turned to Olivia. "Can I take yours, too?" He was so formal with her, so guarded. She'd expected that, but didn't realize how much it would bother her.

Olivia shrugged out of her coat and handed it to him. She could be polite, too. "Thank you."

Mick nodded, then turned back to Will. "I've got a snack cupboard, and I'm pretty sure we can find a soccer game on one of the sports channels."

"I want to stay with you," Will said, his tone pleading as he stared at Olivia.

"I need to talk to Ms. Dalton for a little longer while you watch the game. You'd be totally bored by adult stuff. It won't take long." Mick's voice was firm. Olivia could see how he'd have a good teacher presence.

"Okay." Will frowned, his expression sullen as he stalked to the couch and sat down.

"I'll just get him settled," Mick said apologetically. He walked into the kitchen and came back with arms full of popcorn, protein snacks, and even a bag of chips. He set them on the coffee table in front of the couch along with a bottle of water.

"Let me find a good soccer match," he said as he turned on the TV. After flipping through a few channels, he found a game on.

Will ignored him until he saw the popcorn. When he was munching away, his eyes glued to the screen, Mick motioned for Olivia to precede him into the kitchen. He pulled a chair out from his small dining table and then sat down in the chair next to her.

Olivia folded her arms and rested them on the table. They might as well get down to business. "I worked out a really good placement for Will."

"Listen, I'm sorry about implying that Will might be mine, but I thought it would help Will to be able to stay with me for a while. He likes me. I'm familiar to him. He's safe here. Is there any way we can fast track me through the rest of the red tape so I can be his foster father?" Mick met her eyes. "I want that kid to have better options than he's had in life so far, and I think I could really help him."

Olivia leaned closer, thinking of the files she'd read, including Mick's own foster care experience. "What made you want to be a foster parent?" She didn't want to pry, but she also didn't want to admit that she'd looked into his background. Somehow it seemed better if he volunteered the information.

"I want to give a stable home to kids in need." Mick tilted

back in his chair and folded his arms. "Will already has a loving adult who can take care of him in me. Doesn't that count for something?"

"It does, but there are laws and policies for children in his situation. We can find another safe place for him within those laws." Olivia wanted to reach out, to somehow offer him the reassurance he obviously needed. But what would that even be?

Mick pushed away from the table so abruptly, it startled Olivia. He didn't look at her, though, and went to the sink. "You don't know anything about living in foster care. It's not always a safe place."

Olivia stood closer to him, making sure to leave some distance between them. "We have a place for him in one of the best foster homes in the area. The caseworker and I pulled a lot of strings to get one close enough that you can visit him and keep an eye on things." Her voice was soft, but just as firm as his had been when talking to Will.

Mick gripped the edge of the counter, his head hung low. Sadness mixed with frustration radiated from his entire frame. After a moment, he raised his eyes to hers, the pain visible. "Why can't he stay with me?"

Her heart broke a little at the pleading tone. But he had to know deep down that Will couldn't stay. "You said it yourself, you aren't a licensed foster parent." She softened her voice, knowing her words would be a blow. "You're not his father. You're probably not prepared for a child right now."

"I have a room for him. Money to buy clothes and food. I can offer him a safe place to live and a caring guardian. What more does a child need?" He turned to face her, running both hands through his hair. "There isn't a foster parent out there who could do it better than I could."

"What will you do when he's sick? Take the day off? The elementary school gets out before the high school. Who will pick him up and watch him until your classes are done for the day? He might have disruptive behaviors that present themselves as a result of what he's been through. How will you handle that?" Olivia unfolded her arms and rested her palm on the counter. Every muscle in her body seemed tense, as if she was arguing a case in a courtroom. This wasn't supposed to be confrontational, so she backed off a bit. "There's a lot to think about when you take on a child."

"Don't you believe that I can make adjustments in my life for him?" Mick's brows knit together and he shook his head. "I can, and I will."

Olivia leaned in a bit, but kept her hand splayed on the cool countertop to ground herself. "But what's best for him? Someone who's already trained and ready for him, or someone who's winging it?"

"Someone who cares for him!" Mick pushed off from the counter with an exasperated grunt. He walked to the doorway, as if checking on Will. His concern was evident, but Olivia couldn't cave. She'd found the best solution for all of them, and she needed Mick to see that.

"If you feel that strongly about it, finish your training and become licensed. Then maybe we can reevaluate." Olivia stayed where she was, sensing that Mick needed a little space.

"There's got to be a way I can keep Will." Mick turned to her, his expression hopeful.

"No, there isn't. Will already has a placement waiting for

him. I promise you, I got him the best home I know of." She held Mick's gaze, willing him to see the truth in her eyes. "He'll be happy there."

Mick clenched his fists and broke eye contact. "You don't know that. You have no idea what goes on behind closed doors. On the outside it may be the best home you know of, but inside it could be a house of horrors."

Olivia took a breath. From the pained look on his face, he was reliving the time he spent as a foster child in the Hawkins household. "Listen, I know you didn't have a good experience in foster care, but things have changed since then."

Mick's head whipped up at her words. "What did you say?" He took three steps closer until he was right in front of her. "Have you been spying on me? Digging up dirt on my life? Is that the real reason why I can't keep Will?"

Olivia could feel the fury in every tense muscle of Mick's body. She held her ground, but everything in her wanted to step back. "No, of course not. I had to do a check after releasing a child into your care. Your name popped up on the Hawkins case."

Mick snorted and turned his back to her, throwing an arm up in disbelief. "It's just a case to you. Every official, every social worker, and policeman called that—a case. But it was my life!"

"I'm sorry. I didn't read the file, but I remember the trial and news reports from the criminal case." Olivia bit her lip. The horror this man had lived through would have affected even the most hardened police officer. He'd been starved until he was severely underweight, and beaten so badly that by the time he was rescued, doctors were hard-pressed to find an inch of him that wasn't black and blue. "I'm sure you know that John and

Phyllis Hawkins were sent to prison, and all kinds of safeguards were put in place. Nothing like what you went through will ever happen again."

"You can't guarantee that. No one thought the Hawkins' household was anything other than a safe place for children and look what happened." He turned to meet her gaze, the fury banked, but still visible in his eyes. "I'm sure some kids fall through the cracks, and I don't want to take that chance with Will. Not when I can protect him."

"But that's not your job or your right," she said softly. "It's mine. Let me protect him."

"Did you work all night to make sure he didn't get more than a day with me? I never had a chance." His accusing glare dared her to contradict the words, but she couldn't. Now, seeing how much it meant to him, part of her wished she'd waited.

"I spent a lot of time last night and this morning setting things up, yes." She moved closer. His anger seemed to be dissipating and she could see he was beginning to accept what had to happen. "I want what's best for Will."

"There's nothing I can do to change your mind?" His jaw clenched as he stared at the doorway that led to the living room. "Nothing at all?"

"No, I'm sorry." And she was. But she had a job to do.

He sighed and sat down at the table again, his shoulders slumped. "Tell me about this foster family."

"Their names are Eric and Wendy Jurgens. They've been foster parents for about ten years and have adopted four of their foster kids. Sweet family with a lot of love." She sat across from him. "They can give Will the stability he needs right now, and they've had several children already in similar situations. They've been down this road before, and children really respond to them."

"Are they in town? I don't recognize the name. He won't have to change schools, will he?" Mick asked. The anger seemed to be slowly seeping from him, but there was still tension in his shoulders.

At least he's listening. "No, but he'll have to take the bus. The Jurgens' live on the outskirts of town." She tilted her head. "And he'll have foster brothers to ride with, so you don't have to worry about him being alone."

Mick closed his eyes briefly before looking at her. "I can see why you're a good lawyer. You're pretty persuasive."

Olivia smiled. "I'm going to take that as a compliment." She reached across the table and touched his arm. "I really am trying to look out for Will and his best interests."

"I know. I just got attached to him so quickly, and with my past . . ." His voice trailed off, and he looked down at her hand near his elbow before he pulled away. "I'm not ashamed of my past, just wary when it comes to foster care."

She clasped her hands in her lap. Why had she touched him? She straightened and used her most professional tone. "I deal with a lot of placements, and though they aren't all perfect, the way caseworkers, courts, and families work together for the kids in the system has changed a lot since you were there."

"I'm going to hold you to that." He got up from the chair and pushed it in. "I'll tell Will, if you don't mind. What time are we expected at the Jurgens?"

Olivia looked at her watch, carefully avoiding Mick's gaze. "In about an hour."

"Wow, you don't mess around, do you?" Frustration crept back into his voice. "Couldn't you have given me one more day with him?"

She stood up so he wouldn't be looking down on her anymore. Her head only reached his shoulder, but somehow she felt stronger when they were on a more even level. "Drawn-out goodbyes are hard on everyone and the Jurgens family is eager to meet him."

Without a word he swept past her into the living room. Olivia walked to the window to look outside. She'd give him the space to tell Will, and then they could all head over to meet the Jurgens family. Once Mick met them, his fears would be put to rest. They just had a knack for putting people at ease.

But Mick had only been gone for thirty seconds when he reappeared in the kitchen. "He's gone."

"Gone? What do you mean?" Olivia's brow furrowed. Her mind grasped what he said, but she didn't want to believe it.

"Will must have overheard us talking. He's run away." Mick handed her Will's brand-new coat. "He didn't take this, and it's starting to snow. I'm going to find him."

"I'm coming with you." She grabbed her own coat from an armchair and pulled it on before she followed Mick, her heart in her throat. If anything happened to that little boy . . .

"Let's go," she said, a tremor of fear pushing her through the door.

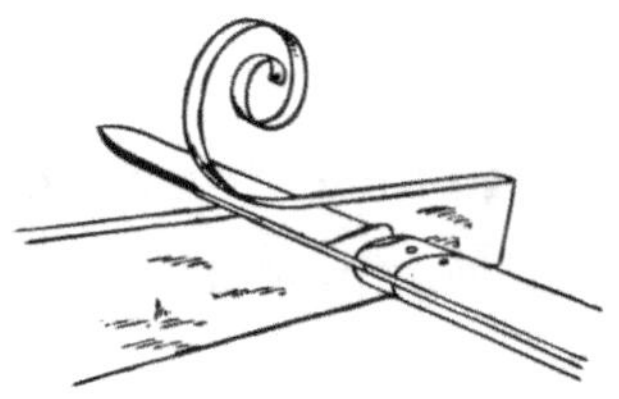

$\mathcal{M}$ick clenched the little coat in his hand before he tossed it into the backseat and slid behind the wheel of his rental car. Olivia got in on the passenger's side and he barely waited for her to buckle up before he drove toward the park he'd found Will in the first time. If he wasn't there, Mick wasn't sure where else to look. His stomach rolled at that thought. There were so many things that could happen to a seven-year-old. Thankfully, Lincoln was a small town, but still. A parent couldn't be too careful.

After they'd parked, Mick grabbed the coat and got out. He wanted to run, but merely picked up the pace in his hurry to search the park. Olivia stayed right behind him and didn't complain. She'd worn a gray sweater and black pants with flats, instead of the heels he'd seen her in before, which made sense since it was the weekend. Did she ever wear jeans? Or have any casual clothes that didn't look like she could be walking into court any minute? Maybe not. When she talked about Will, though, he'd seen genuine concern in her eyes, her lawyer façade finally cracking. At least the boy was definitely more than a job to her.

If she just could have left well enough alone. But Mick knew that wasn't fair. She'd laid out her case quite convincingly that the Jurgens would be the best choice for Will right now, though they needed to find and convince *him* so he wouldn't keep running away.

They finally made it to the far corner of the park, and Mick scanned the playground equipment. No sign of Will. His heart sank. It wasn't snowing heavily, but the temperature was dropping, and the kid only had a t-shirt on.

"Where could he be?" Mick turned to go back the way they'd come. "I thought he'd be here for sure."

Olivia touched his arm, and he felt that little zing pass between them, like it had earlier in his kitchen. Before he could pull away, though, she snatched her hand back as if she'd been burned. Mick tried to catch her eye, to get a clue as to what she was feeling in that moment, but she turned her head.

"Wait," she said softly. "Look over there."

Mick looked in the direction she'd tilted her head, toward the small plastic tunnel closest to them. A small figure sat huddled in the front. "There he is," Mick breathed, gratitude and relief filling him.

He walked over the wood chips that covered the playground, his long strides eating up the distance between them. "Will," he called.

The boy lifted his head and his eyes went wide when he saw Mick and wider when he saw Olivia. He jumped up and tried to run away. Mick quickly caught up to him and grabbed his arm. "Hey, what's going on? Where are you going?"

"I heard you. You don't want me." Will's words choked on a sob. "You're going to send me away."

Mick hugged the little boy to him. His arms were like ice, so Mick pulled the coat around him and rubbed his shoulders to warm him up. "That's not true. I *do* want you, but it's not that simple. If you would have waited a bit longer, I would have explained."

Will stuck his chin out. "You said we would work it out. That you hoped I could stay. Last night in your woodshop."

"And I do want you to stay, but you can't. Ms. Dalton found you a place close by, though, so if you want, I can come and visit you."

Olivia crouched next to them. "The Jurgens family has two boys just a little older than you. And they love sports, too." She reached out to help Will zip up his coat all the way. "I think you'd like it there."

"I like Mick's house." Will's nose was running, and he wiped it on his sleeve. "Why can't I stay with him?"

"I need to take care of a few things first before you're allowed to," Mick said. "The Jurgens are already approved and ready for you."

"You're good at taking care of things." Will looked up at Mick. "Can't I stay with you while you do that?"

Mick wanted so badly to say yes, but he couldn't get Will's hopes up. "No, you can't. There are rules that we have to follow whether we like them or not," he said honestly. "But I'll be over to visit you a lot so you can keep teaching me all your soccer tricks, okay?"

Will still had tears in his eyes and Mick's chest squeezed.

"Okay," Will finally said in a small voice. Why couldn't things have been different?

Olivia seemed to sense Mick needed some back up to stick to the deal. "Will, would you like to go meet the Jurgens family? I hear they have a pretty big yard perfect for soccer."

Will didn't look at her, but took Mick's hand and squared his shoulders. "I guess."

The three of them walked back to the car. Snowflakes were starting to come down a little harder, making Mick grateful they'd found Will when they did. "I was really worried when I couldn't find you, you know."

"I'm sorry." He didn't meet Mick's gaze.

Mick gripped his little hand tighter. "It's okay to want to be alone sometimes, but you should always let people know where you're going."

Will hung his head and his footsteps slowed. "Okay. I'll try."

They were all quiet in the car, except for Olivia's instructions on how to get to the Jurgens' home. When they pulled up to the two-story house, Mick was surprised. It was like a farmhouse from the pictures he'd seen in books as a kid—a big porch with rocking chairs and lots of light spilling from the windows.

"This is it?"

"Yep. I love their porch." Olivia opened the car door. She turned to Will in the back seat. "I know the family is anxious to meet you."

They walked up the stairs to the porch, Will between them. Mick took a deep breath while Olivia knocked. First impressions could tell a lot about a person. What if he had a bad feeling about this? Would Olivia listen to him?

A tall woman with short, spiky brown hair and a big smile opened the door. "Come in, come in," she invited. "I can't believe it's snowing!"

Olivia went first, and Will hung back with Mick. He took Will's hand and they walked into the house, together. They looked around, both of their mouths open in surprise at the scene before them. A fire burned in the fireplace, and two boys were on the couch. It was like a perfect scene from the movies. But Mick knew appearances could be deceiving. He needed more information.

Both of the kids on the couch turned to stare at Will, who promptly moved behind Mick again. He put his arm around the boy's shoulder and gave him a little squeeze. They could do this. The Jurgens family deserved a chance.

Olivia glanced at them, then spoke to the woman who'd opened the door. "I don't know if we've met before. I'm Olivia Dalton. Susan is Will's new caseworker, and when we set everything up, she said it would be okay to just bring him over instead of meeting at the CPS offices."

"Susan passed along the message. She's great with follow-up." The woman bent down to Will's level. "Hi there. I'm Wendy. Do you like chocolate chip cookies? I just took some out of the oven."

Will nodded, but didn't move. One of the boys in the living room, who'd been watching them, scooted off the couch and came to stand in front of Will. "Hi, I'm Joseph. I can show you where the cookies are."

He turned and beckoned for Will to follow, and he did. He

looked back at Mick, though, his eyes uncertain. "I won't leave without saying goodbye," Mick reassured him. "I'm just going to talk to Wendy."

Once the boys were in the kitchen, Mick faced the two women. "I hope it's okay if I visit him often. We've kind of gotten attached over the last couple of days."

"As long as that's okay with the caseworker and we figure out some ground rules. I always think it's good for kids to maintain connections, though." Wendy turned to Olivia. "Are we hopeful that Will might be reunited with his mother?"

"She's running from drug charges at the moment, so that's up in the air. You'll definitely be kept informed." Olivia looked beyond Wendy to the kitchen. "He's been through a lot."

"Don't worry. We'll work on helping him feel secure and safe first of all. Everything else will follow." Olivia looked like she was going to say something more, but Wendy held up her hand. "And if anything comes up, we'll figure it out."

"Can I leave my number with you?" Mick asked. "Just in case he needs me."

Olivia took out a small case from her purse and handed Wendy a white business card. "Here's my card. Mick, why don't you write your number on the back?" She pulled a pen out, too.

Mick dutifully wrote his number down and handed it to Wendy.

"I'm glad Will had someone to help him through the first night without his mom," Wendy said, looking down at the card before glancing up at Mick. "Sometimes we all need a friend."

"Thanks." Mick stared at her open, smiling face. It was so opposite of the woman he'd associated with a foster mother —*his* foster mother. Her cold, angry eyes and cutting words were always front and center in his nightmares and had been for years.

"Is everything okay?" Wendy asked, putting her hand up to her cheek. "Do I have flour on my face or something?"

Mick could feel a hot flush of embarrassment rising on his neck. "No, I'm sorry. You just reminded me of something, that's all." He stepped around her and called for Will.

"Are you leaving already?" Will asked, as he came into view with two cookies in one of his hands.

"I don't want to get in the way of your cookies," Mick told him, moving closer and ruffling his hair. "I'll come back tomorrow, okay? See how you're doing."

"Promise?" Will asked, his eyes worried. "I left my toothbrush at your house. Can you bring it?"

"Sure." He bent down and gave Will a hug. "I'll see you tomorrow after school."

He stepped back, and Wendy took his place, putting her arm around Will's shoulder. "Well, Mick, there might not be any cookies left by tomorrow, but you're welcome to stop by for some hot chocolate anytime."

"It's definitely turning into hot chocolate weather," Olivia said, with a smile. "I'll be in touch."

They said their goodbyes, and before he knew it, Mick was standing on the porch with Olivia. He stared at the door, images of the past running through his mind. The door to his foster home had led to fear and misery. Olivia had been right. It wouldn't be like that for Will.

He turned and started walking to his car. He needed to get home. Maybe find some wood to work with to calm his mind.

Olivia was right behind him. "Is everything okay?"

He didn't answer and kept walking to the car. No, everything was not okay. Even though he hadn't known Will long, he would miss having the kid around. He hadn't realized how quiet his house had been until Will had walked into it. Now it would be quiet again. But that was how he liked it, right?

He opened his car door, and Olivia grabbed his arm. "Hey, what's going on here? Will you talk to me?"

"What is there to say?" He looked down at her, soft snowflakes falling in her hair. She looked radiant with the tiny sparkles all over her head. Someone like him, who lived with shadows and black corners, shouldn't be around people like her. He needed to go home. "You were right. I think this is a great placement for Will. Wendy seems capable and loving, everything a foster kid would want."

He moved so he could get in the car, but she covered his fingers gripping the door. Her hand was warm on his, and that heat radiated up his arm. "Everything you didn't get."

"Yes." His emotions felt raw. He needed to get away, to be alone. But Olivia held him there with her hand on his, her eyes looking into his soul.

"I'm sorry," she whispered before she reached up on her tiptoes and pulled him into a hug.

He stiffened at first, not wanting pity, but her arms tightened around him, her warmth like a blaze of light in the darkness. He held her close, wanting to feel that light a little longer. When she started to shiver in his arms, the cold seeping through both of them, he knew he had to get her back to her car.

He pulled away just enough to see her face, her eyes full of kindness staring back at him. He'd always stayed away from emotional attachments. They never ended well, but standing there in the snow with Olivia, for the first time in his life he felt a pull toward another human being. It was a strange feeling, one he wasn't sure what to do with. "Thanks," he finally said, unable to look away from her.

She smiled and pushed her hair out of her eyes. "You're welcome." Turning, she walked around the car to the passenger side. They both got in, and Mick turned up the heater.

They didn't talk all the way back to his house. But it was a good silence, as if she knew he needed a little quiet time to sift through everything.

When he pulled into his driveway and turned off the car, she twisted in her seat to face him. "If you ever need someone to talk to, I'm a great listener."

"That's not what I hear about lawyers," he said, his mouth quirking up in a smile.

"Well, if you ever call me, I'll try to be on my best behavior." She held out her card. "Here's my cell number." She looked at him for a few seconds more, as if silently emphasizing her words. As soon as he took the card from her, she got out of the car.

Mick sat there until she'd driven away, turning her card over and over in his hands. He'd gotten women's numbers before, each one a little victory. But this time, he didn't have to ask for it. Getting Olivia's number had felt right, as if some little puzzle piece had clicked into place. It was unsettling and thrilling at the same time. She knew too much about him, and he wanted to know more about her. And this little card gave him the opportunity to do just that.

He let out a breath. Would he call her? He wanted to. But

she knew things about him, and she'd seen emotions he'd rather not have anyone see.

With all those thoughts swirling through his mind, Mick got out of the car and walked around to the back of the house, still carrying the card. The only thing he wanted right now was to get to his workshop and the wood that could soothe his doubts and anxieties. Where Olivia was concerned, he definitely had a lot of thinking to do.

CHAPTER EIGHT

Olivia worked through lunch on a multiple homicide case and wished she hadn't. The crime scene photos were detailed, but she could compartmentalize the horror in front of her eyes. Today, the thing getting in her head was seeing the pattern and organization of the killer. The disregard for human life and what the killer forced the victims to endure before death was impossible to understand and she didn't want to. But, in order to do her job, she still had to know every inch of the case inside and out, no matter how gruesome, so she slogged on. By three she'd been frustrated with herself and curt with Jana for the better part of the afternoon, so instead of giving her assistant any more reasons to quit, she took a break and went to the sandwich shop across the street.

The cold air in her face as she walked to the diner helped clear her head and drive away the darkness lurking on the edges of her being. Every tough case made that shadow closer and blacker somehow. Pushing it back took a little longer.

When she opened the door and stepped into the diner, the familiarity of it made her spirits feel a bit lighter, though.

It didn't take long before she had her favorite grilled chicken sandwich in front of her and after a few bites she felt calmer, her hangry impulse quelled. Lingering over the last of her sandwich, she didn't want to go back to the office and the case files just yet. She let her mind revisit the hug she'd shared with Mick and analyze it again. He'd seemed so wooden in her arms at first, but just before Olivia let him go, he pulled her so close she could hardly breathe. Her heart had beat triple time as she'd closed her eyes and enjoyed having his arms around her. The connection between them was strong and undeniable, but as they'd pulled apart, she'd seen a haunted look in his eye for a split second before he shuttered his emotions. How was she supposed to interpret that?

She'd already explored several options of what that glimpse of bleakness could mean as she picked at her sandwich. Her brain wandered from the hug down the path of whether Mick's eyes were a cloudy sky sort of blue or a stormy ocean blue, but her cell phone ringing brought her back to the present. She pulled the phone out of her pocket, and swallowed before picking up. "Hello?"

"Olivia, it's Mick." His voice sounded smooth, but there was a hint of roughness to it. Did she make him nervous? The idea sent a little thrill through her.

"Hey, I didn't expect to hear from you so soon." She used her professional voice, in case he was calling about Will, but her mind was still contemplating what color his eyes were, and how she hadn't wanted that hug to end. Locking those thoughts away so she didn't sound like a breathless schoolgirl, she focused on something practical and right in front of her by gathering the garbage from her table and putting it on her tray. "Is everything okay?"

There was a beat of silence before he said, "I went over to visit Will yesterday, as promised, but they've asked me to give him a bit of space to get to know his new foster family." He paused, and her heart went out to him. Was he upset about that? "It's been harder than I imagined, and I thought you might have some suggestions for me."

"You're asking me for suggestions to keep busy?" For some reason, that amused her. She was the workaholic. No one ever asked her for entertainment ideas.

"Have you been to Pebble Cove? Maybe you could take a walk with me as far as the hot springs. It's too cold to swim or anything, but it's got some nice views. And we can talk." He was silent for a moment, and seemed out of breath when he added, "about Will."

She let his words sink in. Walk with him. To the hot springs. Her heart skipped a beat. "So is this a date or are you asking me as a professional to talk you through the transition with Will?" She balled the sandwich wrap in her palm until it was no bigger than a quarter.

Mick cleared his throat. "A date. If you want it to be."

A smile started to curl her lips upward, but she pressed them together. This could get complicated. On the other hand, she hadn't been able to stop thinking about him, and here was her chance to explore things a bit further. "What time and should I meet you at the trailhead?"

"I can pick you up at home if you like," he offered.

"No, that's an extra hour's worth of driving for you. How

about I just meet you at my brother's house? That way you won't have to leave town." She stood and took her tray to the garbage. "What time?"

"Would five work for you at all? Then we'd be in time to catch the sunset." He sounded more confident now. How many women had he taken to the hot springs to talk? The thought of him up there with someone else burst her happiness bubble for a minute, but she pushed it away.

"Perfect." She bit her lip, thinking of the mountain of paperwork she still had to minimize somehow, but really, there wasn't anything that couldn't wait until tomorrow. And it had been a long time since she'd had fluttery feelings about a first date. "I'll see you then."

"See you then. Oh, and wear something warm, especially gloves." He had a hint of laughter in his voice.

"Why *especially* gloves?" Her tone turned suspicious. Was this some sort of test?

He chuckled, his rich baritone resonating through her. "Didn't you say your hands get ice cold when you're nervous?"

That cockiness she'd seen when she'd first been introduced to him at the school's costume ball last year had definitely returned. She used her best lawyer voice, which always put witnesses on edge. "Why on earth would I be nervous?"

"Because you're going on a date with me." Self-confident and brash, but not overbearing. Part of her liked seeing that again after the vulnerability he'd shown over Will. He hadn't lost it or withdrawn into himself.

"You know, Mick, maybe it's you who should be nervous. I'm a pro at first dates. They're old hat. Nothing to be worried about. You, on the other hand, have a reputation for knowing all the best trails in the Lincoln foothills."

According to Drew, Mick mapped a lot of the trails himself so he never took a date on the same walk twice. And since he dated a lot, and apparently loved to hike, that meant he must know a lot of trails. Or maybe Drew had been wrong, and Mick only used the trail to the hot springs for dates. Her face heated at the possibility of being just one woman of many who made that trek. Regardless, she wanted to spend time with him, whether he was taking her to his regular date spot that he'd taken a dozen girls to or not. She was hoping to know him better, the Mick he didn't show to everyone, and this was the first step.

His voice went low, as if he'd pulled the phone closer and read her thoughts. "I'm sensing a little hesitation on your part. Are you nervous I'll live up to whatever stories your brother has told you?"

She'd just exited the deli, but stopped mid-stride as a little shiver went through her. Her brother *had* told her stories of Mick's charm and prowess. She herself had seen small glimpses of his laughter and smiles with Will. How would he be as a date? "There have been quite a few stories about you. Some that were hard to believe."

Mick chuckled. "Probably true, then. But your brother also talks about you." His voice was velvet and warmth pulsed through her veins all the way to her toes.

"Oh yeah? Well, I won't claim all his stories are true." She started walking again, but kept the phone close to her ear, as if that would keep him close.

"I'd definitely like to find out," he murmured. "See you at five."

She couldn't wipe the smile off of her face as she disconnected, but at the same time, thought about calling Drew. What had he said about her? He had so much dirt from her childhood and teen years. This could be really fun or horribly disastrous. She was hoping for fun.

Olivia hurried the rest of the way to her office, barely noticing the people around her. Walking in, all she could think about was getting straight to her computer so she could tie up some loose ends on the murder file she'd worked on all day, then she could head home to change. What would she wear?

Jana came into her office with a file in her hand. "Here are the copies you requested."

"Thanks. Listen, I'm sorry about before." She leaned over her desk. "You are worth your weight in gold around here. I hope you know that."

Jana nodded. "It's okay. Know what? Leave early today. Get some rest. You've been working twelve-hour days for weeks on the Tunston murders. I think it's catching up to you."

"You're right. I'll finish up this motion and head home. Thanks." Olivia swiveled her chair to face her computer. Her thoughts turned back to the weekend and Mick's eyes fixed on hers after their hug. Had she imagined the spark between them? Would it happen again tonight?

"You're actually taking my advice?" Jana asked, her hands on her hips and both eyebrows raised. "Has that ever happened before?"

"Yes," Olivia said when Jana gave her 'the look.' "Okay, not usually when it comes to quitting time, but almost every other advice you give." She tilted her head and gave a little shrug. "You're right and I know it. I need some downtime." And a chance to see if her attraction to Mick was because of his love for a little boy or something more.

She finished up as quickly as possible and went home to change. After putting on her jeans that were comfortable and still looked good on her, and combining it with a red flannel shirt and a ponytail, she gave herself a critical once-over. Practical, yet pretty. And definitely warm enough for a mountain hike. She hesitated as she put on her coat. Should she bring the gloves? Mick was right; more than likely her hands would be ice cold and gloves would help that. But he might think he'd won the challenge if she did. She stuffed them in her pockets, out of sight, but there just in case. Shaking her head, Olivia smiled. She was definitely overthinking this.

The trip down to Lincoln didn't take long and she pulled up to her brother's house in record time. With five minutes to spare, she debated even knocking on her brother's door since she wouldn't have time to visit with him or his family. But she didn't have to debate long, because there was Drew, striding toward her car. He was frowning at something in the distance, and Olivia turned around to see what he was looking at. Her heart sank. Mick had gotten out of his car.

She opened her door and intercepted Drew. "Hey, I was just coming to knock on your door."

"Mick beat you to it. Said he was meeting you here." Drew folded his arms, disapproval practically dripping off of him. "You seriously have a date with him?"

"You didn't believe me?" Mick asked as he stopped next to her.

"I want to hear it from my sister." Drew looked pointedly at her, the expression he'd used her entire life when she'd done something he didn't approve of. "Liv, can I talk to you in private for a moment?"

Olivia glanced at Mick, then moved off a few paces. Drew made it a few more, and she noticed he'd come out in socks, but no shoes. He must have been more upset than she thought. "You can't be serious."

"Why not?" Olivia frowned, barely stopping herself from looking back at Mick. "We're just hiking up to the hot springs and watching the sunset." She put her hand on his arm, trying to soothe his obviously ruffled feathers. "It's no big deal."

"My baby sister going out with Mick *is* a big deal. He's broken the heart of nearly every single female in the school, if not the town. He's a serial dater, and when he gets tired of a woman, he drops her like a hot potato. I don't want that for you." Drew bent down to catch her eye. "I don't want you to get hurt."

Olivia kissed him on the cheek. "You're a good big brother, but I've got this, okay? Don't wait up for me." She smiled as she walked back to Mick. But Drew wasn't giving up so easily. He was right on her heels.

"Hey, Mick," he started, his voice barely above a growl. "Do I need to say it?"

Mick held up a hand. "You don't have anything to worry about, Drew. I'll have her home by midnight." He turned, but Olivia caught the, "Dad," Mick muttered under his breath. She stifled a laugh and averted her eyes. If she looked at Drew now, she wouldn't be able to hold it in and pushing her brother's limits was not a good idea at the moment.

"Time to go." Olivia rolled her eyes and nearly pushed Mick to his car. He helped her into her seat, and as he went around to the driver's side, she noticed Drew hadn't moved, and was standing on the curb glowering at them.

She sighed and gave *him* the pointed look. In the courtroom, she faced down murderers and hardened felons, so while Drew's concern came from a place of love, she could take care of herself. He ought to know that by now.

Mick got in and they both watched Drew for a few seconds before he finally walked back into his house. "Should I be worried?"

"About a date with me? Or Drew?" She tilted her head and raised an eyebrow.

"Never mind," Mick said, as he started the car. "I'll take my chances with both."

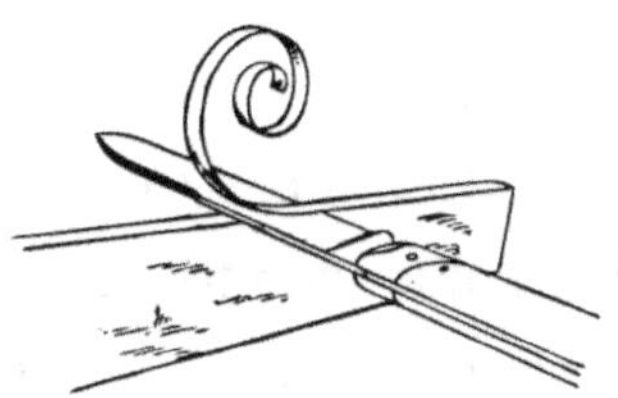

ick had hiked the path to the hot springs many times before, but today felt different. He watched Olivia a few paces ahead. Her steps were sure, but every now and then, she sent him a glance that made *him* feel a bit off balance. Her hair swung in a ponytail behind her, just brushing her shoulders as she walked. He'd mostly seen her with her hair up and for a second he imagined himself taking it down and running his fingers through the length. The image was so powerful, his hand reached out, but he yanked it back, glad she was in front of him and hadn't noticed.

The force of their connection had caught him off-guard, but combined with the fact that she knew things no one else did about him, made him vulnerable. Other women had only ever seen what he wanted them to see, but Olivia had drawn back the curtains. How was he supposed to deal with that? Every sense was heightened as he watched closely for reactions from her that would prove she was going to leave or pity him in some way. So far she hadn't given him any indications, but this hike might bring out her true thoughts.

He caught up to her as they reached a fork in the path. "So, tell me more about yourself."

She lifted a corner of her mouth in a half-smile as she looked over at him. "That's your best line?"

He chuckled at her boldness in calling him out. "Well, I thought I'd work up to those." He held a tree branch out of the way so she could pass. "I do want to get to know you better, though. All I've got is what Drew's told me."

Olivia abruptly stopped walking. "So, he talks about me at school? I can't really picture how I would come up."

"We were in the break room, and Mrs. Sorensen was saying how she'd seen the new *Star Wars* movie twice over the weekend, and wouldn't mind seeing it fifty more times, it was so good." He grinned as the realization of what he was going to say next stole over her face.

Olivia closed her eyes and let out a groan. "He didn't."

"Apparently *you've* seen *Top Gun* over fifty times and can quote the whole thing." Mick bent down to look into her eyes. "So, do you have a thing for Maverick or Ice Man? Or is it Goose?"

Olivia stood still for a moment, her hands clenching and unclenching before she stalked past him, her feet grinding the leaves and dirt on the path. "I'm going to kill my brother."

Mick followed, not quite ready to let the subject drop. "Hey, it's not that bad. I was just surprised by the movie choice. That's a pretty old one."

"It's a classic," Olivia threw over her shoulder. "And I'm

surprised *you* haven't seen it, especially since there's a romance that starts with one terrible pick-up line."

"Who says I haven't seen it?" He stopped and held his hand over his heart. *"You never close your eyes anymore when I kiss your lips,"* he sang, his voice ringing out over the trees.

Olivia turned around and stared. "You've seen *Top Gun?*"

"More than once. But I'd say the storyline is more than a romance with a bad pickup line. It's an awe-inspiring action film with a great bromance." He started walking again, and she fell into step beside him.

"I can quote all those bromance lines," Olivia said, quirking her eyebrow at him. "Now that you know my favorite movie, what's yours? Or are you only an action-film connoisseur?"

"I think every guy is into action films. But my favorite movie would have to be Disney's *Aladdin.*" She snorted, and he held up his hand at her obvious disbelief. "It really is! I knew I shouldn't have told you."

"Your favorite movie is *Aladdin.* A children's movie." Doubt threaded through her tone and she was obviously trying to hold in a smile. "I'm surprised at *your* choice, that's all. What do you like best about it? The three wishes thing?"

"Well, if a genie appeared, I'd have some ideas for him, but no, that's not why I like it." He tilted his head toward her. "You probably didn't even realize that it has one of the greatest pickup lines of all time."

Olivia's forehead wrinkled. "None come to mind."

They were at the turnoff where the rocks and hillside hid the hot springs. He could hear water gurgling a few hundred feet ahead and didn't want to get there just yet, in case they wouldn't be alone. He stopped and leaned against the rocks, grateful that the little snowstorm they'd had on Saturday had melted. The temperature was perfect for hiking. Olivia stopped and turned to face him.

He took a breath. "I don't know if I should tell you all my secrets." Mick was smiling, as if he wasn't quite serious, but there was a bit of truth to his words. His secrets, his past, were all part of his armor. He didn't want anyone to get close, especially someone like Olivia—strong, independent. All of the things he wanted to make sure people thought he was, but that she might not.

"I wouldn't consider sharing a pickup line a secret. More like a warning." She stepped closer until the toes of their boots were nearly touching. "What's the line?"

He looked down into her eyes, luminous in the fading light. She didn't seem to have any of the shadows that he carefully hid with careless fun and numerous dates. He leaned close, breathing in the clean scent that surrounded her. In the trees, with the rock wall at his back, it felt like they were the only two people in the world. "When Aladdin reaches down to Jasmine, and he says, 'Do you trust me?'" His voice was lower than he intended on those last four words, making it seem as if he were really asking her the question.

The air around them charged, and his gaze dropped to her lips. A perfect pink. As if Olivia was following his line of thought, she bit her bottom lip and lifted her chin. So accessible. He reached up to touch her hair, but as soon as he moved, she took a step backward, and the spell was broken.

"Oh yeah. That's a good one," she said, her voice catching. She cleared her throat. "Thanks for the warning." She slowly turned around and started walking again.

Mick watched her go down the path for a minute, wanting to call to her, to take it all back. He knew touching her hair, wanting to kiss her, was too much, but her warmth called to the coldness in his core that had been there for as long as he could remember. All the more reason to put his walls back in place.

Don't get close. People never stay.

He followed her to the springs. She'd chosen a large rock to sit on near the far side, where the water molded into a shallow basin barely bigger than a hot tub. It was a popular place with the townspeople, but at the moment, Olivia and Mick were alone. He chose a rock a little ways away and started to take off his boots. When he was barefoot, he rolled up his pant legs, stuck his feet in the water, and leaned back. The hot spring was just the thing he needed. He closed his eyes, but could hear Olivia unlacing her boots and the small splash her feet made as she joined him.

"I'm sorry," she said softly. "I'm sure you're used to coming up here with women and flirting and kissing. But when I kiss someone, it means something to me."

He didn't open his eyes. "You don't have to explain anything to me. I get it."

"Do you?" Her voice was closer. She'd leaned forward. "I want to get to know the real Mick. The one who cares about a little abandoned boy he hardly knows. The Mick who survived a childhood no one should have ever had to live through and who became a man with compassion and empathy in his heart."

He didn't want to look at her. Her words pierced him, but he didn't recognize the man she described. If she knew the real him, she wouldn't want to get close. The things he'd survived had left so many scars. If he let her in, she would see the ugliness—the shadows and darkness where his heart should have been. No, it was better if he kept her on the outside.

"I think you've mistaken me for someone else." He turned away, dipping his feet a little farther in. "I'm a teacher. It's my job to care about kids."

He could feel her watching him, so he met her gaze. Lies were better believed if you looked them in the eye when you said them.

"It's more than that with Will, and you know it." She took her feet out and wrapped her arms around her knees. "I'm not going to ask you about your past. But if you want to share, I'm here." She pushed some stray hair that had escaped her ponytail behind her ear and stared down at the rock she was sitting on. "With my job, I've seen a lot of things I wish I could unsee. Sometimes I have to close my feelings off, box up my heart into a tiny corner of my mind just so I can sleep through the night without seeing victims' faces haunting my dreams. And I think that's what you do, too."

The decades-old ache welled up inside him as her voice and what she was saying sank into his soul. Inch by inch, she was cracking open his hidden box of feelings, but he willed himself to close it again. He couldn't let her see the real him, couldn't allow her to see his fear that he was unlovable. She'd never understand and he didn't want to look too close.

"This isn't about seeing something bad at work. This is about what I lived through. I'm one of those kids in your criminal files because of what happened to me. You look at me as another victim. You see the aftermath of what I lived through, but you've never been on that side." And that was also why they could never be together.

He wouldn't be the victim. Ever.

She stared at him as if he were speaking another language. "I don't look at you as a victim, and just because I haven't experienced what you have, doesn't mean I've never suffered in my life. It doesn't mean that I can't relate or understand how your childhood shaped you."

"You can relate to my childhood?" He laughed, but it sounded brittle. "From what your perfect brother has said, you were raised with two parents who loved you. You've always had an older brother to protect you if anyone looked at you wrong." He grabbed his boots, frustration welling in him. "You don't understand the first thing about me. You can't relate. You can't fix me." He awkwardly shoved his feet into his socks and laced up his boots as quickly as he could.

"You're deliberately misunderstanding me," Olivia said, struggling to put her own damp feet into her socks. "Do you know why I've watched *Top Gun* fifty times? The real reason? Because if I don't do my job well enough, a defendant can go free, even if I feel it in my bones they're guilty and know they're going to hurt someone else. There's nothing I can do. I failed. So I sit and watch that movie to live in a make-believe world for a couple of hours where the good guys always win."

Mick could see she was shaking as she laced up her boots. He opened his mouth to say something, but she shook her head and pointed a finger at his chest.

"Do you know what's waiting for me on my desk at work? Crime scene photos of four murder victims who were tortured before they were killed. And I get to try and put their killer away for life—to sit in the same room with him while we go over every detail until I want to scream inside. *That's* the darkness I deal with on a daily basis." Her voice dropped low and she pegged him with her gaze. "We all have shadows and darkness to deal with. It's how you do it that counts."

He'd never seen such raw emotion from someone and didn't know how to react. Part of him wanted to apologize and reach out to her, but she was so infuriated, he wasn't sure if he should. He stood and held out his hands in front of him. "What do you want from me?"

"I wanted you to take a chance, but you obviously can't do that, so now I want you to take me home. This date is over." She walked past him without a backward glance.

He followed, an apology on the tip of his tongue, but he didn't say it. So many feelings were swirling through him. It awed him that she had similar demons to wrestle, but at the same time, he was stunned. She seemed happy and light whenever he'd been around her. For him, sometimes it felt like a full-time job to keep the soul-wrenching blackness at bay and he had to work hard to find the joy. Hearing someone describe their experience, though, was eye-opening. Maybe he'd been too quick to judge, but just because they had similar demons to deal with, didn't make them compatible.

He watched her walk away, her back straight, marching so fast they'd make it down to his car in half the time. But even with the similarities, the bottom line was, they were still too different. He'd never know what it was like to prosecute criminals and she wouldn't know what it was like to live with one. They were at an impasse. And from the way she was ending this date, probably a permanent one.

He followed her down the path, the silence between them saying more than words ever could.

CHAPTER TEN

Olivia couldn't stop reliving her date with Mick two weeks ago. She'd revealed more about herself than she ever intended, but she wasn't sorry. Hopefully it had given him something to think about. But it was the near-kiss that had shaken her. She'd never wanted to give in so badly as she had in that moment. Only the thought of him taking a dozen other girls up there to make out with them stopped her. She wasn't going to be his next conquest. Though, the small glimpses she'd seen that there was more to him than that tantalized her, except there was no sign he would ever trust her enough to share that part of him.

Tapping her fingers on her desk, she stared at the brief in front of her. She'd read it through three times, but couldn't concentrate. The workday had been crawling by. With a glance at the clock, she was surprised to see it was only noon. At least five hours to go.

Usually she was so busy that noon came and went with

barely any notice. Ever since she'd started talking to Mick Donovan, though, her normal routine had gone out the window. Rubbing the back of her neck, she decided to take a break. Food might lift her mood a little and get her through the rest of the day. After grabbing her purse out of the locked drawer in her desk, she let Jana know she was going to her favorite sandwich shop across the street, but if anything came up, to call her.

As she left the office, the cold air outside hit her full force. It didn't clear her mind, just left her cold, and Olivia pulled her coat closer around her. The temperature was starting to feel more like winter than fall. Hurrying across the street, she was grateful there wasn't a line at the deli. She opened the door and stepped into its warmth.

The guy behind the counter smiled. "Your usual?"

"Yes, thanks." She leaned against the counter to wait while he made her a loaded turkey club. Sometimes it was nice to have someone know what you like without having to tell them.

Once she had her food, she sat at her usual table near the window and pulled out her phone. With everything Mick churning through her mind, she needed to talk to someone, and her sister-in-law Tori was the perfect person.

"Hey, Tori," Olivia said as soon as she answered. "Are you still in your prep period?"

"Yeah. I've got fifteen minutes before my next class. Is every-thing all right?" Tori asked, paper rustling in the background. "You never call me in the middle of the day."

"I needed to ask you something." Olivia picked at the plastic on her sandwich wrap. "Tell me what you know about Mick. Not about his dating life," she added hastily. "But as a person."

"O-okay." She drew out the word. "He's well-liked by the students. He's a good teacher and really skilled at woodworking. He has a good heart, no matter what anyone says. When I had a panic attack last year, he was right there and knew how to help me through it."

"What do you mean?" Olivia asked. "How did he help you through it?"

"He knew breathing exercises and some focus techniques so I could calm myself down enough to get home." Tori hesitated. "I don't know anything for sure, but with the knowledge he had, I think he's either had panic attacks himself or is close to someone who does."

That would make sense with his background. "I'm glad he was able to help you," Olivia said, finally. "I hadn't heard about that."

Tori was quiet for a moment, then said, "Why all the questions? Drew mentioned you had a date a couple of weeks ago. How did it go?"

"About as expected." Olivia didn't really want to talk about how great it had started—or how badly it ended. Mick had taken her back to her car and they barely said more than two words to each other. "I left early, actually."

"Did he try to kiss you?"

Olivia's face heated, and she was glad Tori couldn't see her. She hadn't ever remembered Tori asking for any details of her dating life before. Drew was obviously rubbing off on her. "Did you kiss Drew on your first date?" It was a lame deflection, but all she could come up with on spur-of-the-moment.

Tori chuckled at the obvious change of subject. "Okay, you don't have to tell me anything."

"It's complicated," Olivia said, not wanting to hurt Tori's feelings. "We probably won't go out again though. It was a one-time thing."

"Drew was sure he was going to have to read Mick the Riot Act. I was glad he didn't." Tori sounded sympathetic. "He paced a lot that night."

"Drew needs to stop being such a worrywart. I thought I saw something in Mick, but I was fooling myself, I guess." She closed her eyes. "I don't know." Her gut still said she wasn't wrong. There was more to Mick than he allowed people to see, but was it worth waiting for?

"You aren't fooling yourself." Tori's voice was soft. Olivia had to press the phone closer to her ear to hear what she was saying. "Mick was a good friend to me when I needed one. He's definitely a keeper for the right woman."

But was Olivia the right woman? The one that he would let in and show all of himself to, both the good and bad? That was the question she had no answers to.

Lost in thought, she'd let the silence go on a bit too long. "Hey, thanks, Tori. Maybe we can all get together for lunch next week?"

"Liv, you can call me anytime. You don't have to wait for a lunch date." The noise in the background was starting to get louder. Tori's prep period was over.

"I'm so glad my brother married you," Olivia said, wishing Tori was standing in front of her so she could give her a hug. "See you soon."

She disconnected the call and unwrapped her sandwich, thinking about what Tori said. Mick was well-liked and had been a true friend to Tori. That reinforced what she'd originally thought. Mick had survived a horrific childhood and had gone on to become an honorable man who worked to help those around him. True, he was a serial dater, but some of that puzzle was falling into place for her. And she hadn't mistaken the haunted look in his eye. Could he ever get over the scars of his past to build a real relationship?

She took a drink of her lemonade. Mick hadn't had any idea of how similar they were in how they dealt with the unimaginable things they'd been forced to witness. She'd shocked him at the hot springs. Her frustration had been too close to the surface with the murder case at the forefront of her work life, but she'd wanted him to see that even with a happy childhood, her career had brought unexpected consequences. Every case she'd worked became part of her, the painful ones turning into part of the darkness that threatened to shadow her soul. Always lurking. But she worked hard to push it away. She'd built walls and created masks to show the world that she was okay, just as he had. But she'd glimpsed behind his façade, and he was running from the part of him that had been revealed. Which was exactly why she wouldn't force anything. Feeling vulnerable was never a good place to start a relationship. *He* needed to want to take a chance.

She finished her sandwich and cleared her table before heading back to work. Time to put Mick out of her mind and get her head back in the game. Her calendar was full, and she had enough work to keep her busy 24/7. Burying herself in work had always helped to push her personal life to the side. That's what she needed to do.

Olivia walked back into the lobby, not as refreshed as she thought she'd be, but at least with some energy to finish out the day. She pulled her badge out as she approached the security door, but stopped short when she heard her name.

"Olivia." David Sullivan stood up and crossed the room to her, bending in as if he was going to give her a kiss on her cheek. She dodged him. "I've been waiting for you."

He sounded vaguely annoyed, but Olivia didn't care. "What did you need, David?" She paused for a moment, but kept her security badge in hand as a hint that she was in a hurry.

"I have a legal problem that I want to talk to you about." He looked around before he leaned closer and smiled. "It's personal."

Olivia groaned inwardly. Maybe she'd get rid of him sooner if she listened to him and sent him on his way. "I only have a few minutes," she warned. Holding up her badge, Olivia went through security and didn't wait to see if he followed. He did. They walked through the assistant's area, and Jana raised her eyebrows as they passed.

Olivia went into her office and walked behind her desk to sit down, thinking that David would sit in the chair opposite. He didn't. Instead, he followed to her side of the desk and sat on the edge, crowding her. The sooner she could get rid of him, the better.

"Okay, David, what's your personal legal matter?"

He splayed his fingers on her desk, as if he were posing for a picture, before he looked down at her. "I can't stop thinking about you. I mean, if being hot were a crime, you'd be guilty as charged." His eyes bored into her, but his silky voice didn't move her in the least. She almost wanted to laugh.

"David, I'm not interested." She put on her game face and folded her hands in her lap. She couldn't be any clearer.

He made a clucking noise. "Yes, you are. I'm the person who makes your life interesting. Without me, all you're stuck with is work." He took a pencil off her desk and rolled it between his fingers. "I'm happy to help. We can have a mutually beneficial relationship. I help you have a little fun and well, you help me by letting me look at you from across the table."

His conceit apparently had no boundaries. Olivia could not believe she'd ever agreed to even one date with this man.

She stood up and he did, too. The smile on his face told her that he thought she'd come to her senses. "David, let me be completely clear. While I appreciate your honesty, I'm not interested. We are not compatible. At all."

"You don't mean that. We had a good time together, didn't we?" He reached out to touch her face, but she held up her hand to ward him off. He pulled away with a condescending shake of his head as if she were a naughty child.

"*You* had a good time handing out your number to the waitresses." He looked down with a faint trace of guilt, but she continued. "When I go out, I expect my date to refrain from flirting with other women." She waited until he met her eyes, wanting what she was saying to get through to him. "It's a big turn-off."

David tilted his head and his eyes widened, as if he was surprised by her answer. She stared back, her gaze unyielding. He knew exactly what she was talking about. Finally, he held up his hands in mock surrender. "Okay, okay, have it your way. But what if I said it won't happen again? Give me another chance. I hate to think of you sitting home alone again, night after night, when I'm totally willing to have some fun together."

"No thank you." She took the pencil out of his hand. He

caught her fingers and flashed her his signature smile, the one that showed off his perfect teeth. *Ugh.* She pulled her hand away and dropped it to her side. "Thanks for coming in."

He looked down at her, his smile fading a little. "I have a feeling I'll be seeing you sooner than you think."

"Don't bet on it."

He gave her a little wave as he left. She could hear him saying something to Jana in his syrupy sweet voice. Hopefully he wasn't trying to come on to her or get her number. Chances were that Jana would see right through him. She usually had a sixth sense about people.

Olivia sat down, feeling a little out of sorts. He'd seemed so sure of her. What would have given him the impression that she would be the kind of woman desperate enough to call him just to avoid being alone?

Putting her head in her hands, she closed her eyes. Mick's face came to mind, crowding out David's. Mick's blue eyes searching hers, crinkling when he laughed with her, the intensity of them when he'd been about to kiss her. With a sigh, she knew it might take more than work to get him out of her mind.

Maybe if she ever got through the rest of today, she'd go visit Will. He'd had two weeks to settle in. And he was a little connection to Mick. Of course, she wouldn't mention him, but no matter what happened with her and Mick, she could still make sure Will was doing okay.

And that might have to be enough, no matter how Olivia wished things were different.

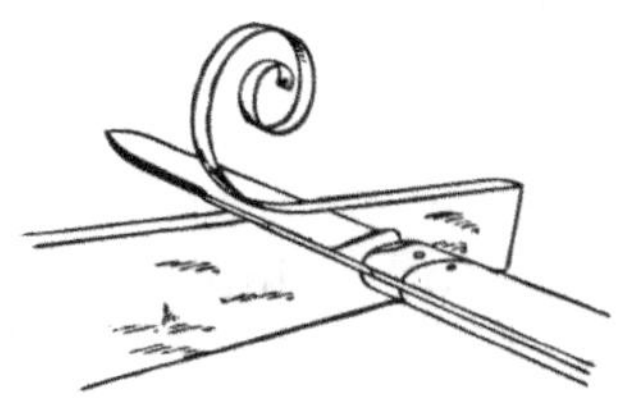

CHAPTER ELEVEN

*M*ick stared at the vending machine in the teacher's lounge. He usually went for the healthier choices, but today, all he wanted was a donut. A messy, sugar-riddled, donut. He put in the dollar bill and picked up the package of six little powdered, round bites of joy. Sitting down at the table, he unwrapped them and ate the first one whole. Two weeks. That's how long it had been since he'd gotten to know Will and Olivia. And they were all he could think about.

The door opened, ending his solitude when Karissa Mead walked in. She'd started teaching the same year he had, and they'd gone out a few times. She'd been pretty hung up on Drew Dalton, though, so he hadn't pursued any more dates with her. He could only take listening to how great Drew was for so long.

"Hey, Karissa," he said, and took another bite of his donut. His mood was starting to lift already. Nothing like a sugar rush.

She sat down in the chair right next to his, her eyes going between him and the donut package. "I'm guessing you're having a rough day. Maybe a rough week."

"Why do you ask?" Mick narrowed his eyes. There was pity in her face. Had she heard something about him and Will? Or Olivia?

"Well . . ." She shifted guiltily in her seat. "I overheard a couple of students saying that you've got some drama going on."

"Drama?" He finished off a third donut and thought about buying another package.

"The story I heard is that you had a secret baby with a female convict who escaped prison and came here looking for you so she could surprise you with the kid and then dump him on you." Karissa held up a hand when he shook his head. "Give me a little credit, Mick. I didn't believe all of it, but I did wonder if there was a kernel of truth to it."

He sighed, grabbing a napkin to wipe his fingers. Sugar wasn't going to help him deal with rumors on top of real life. There probably wasn't enough wood he could carve, either. Maybe a long hike would do the trick.

"None of it's true, actually. I don't have a secret baby, there's no prison escapee, and no one gave me their child." But he still wished the last one could have been true. At least he'd get to visit Will today.

Mrs. Eliason came in with Drew Dalton right behind her. She had a broad smile on her face. "I was so happy when you asked for my family recipe for banana nut bread that I brought you in a loaf. It had to be refrigerated, though." She shuffled over to the fridge and Drew sat down at the table. His presence effectively shut down the conversation with Karissa and Mick, for which he was grateful. He couldn't bear to tell her or anyone what had happened with Will. Not yet.

Mrs. Eliason didn't stick around after she handed Drew the loaf and said a quick hello/goodbye to everyone at the table. Mick managed to smile at her, but his headache was getting stronger with Drew's pointed stare aiming at him. He doubted Olivia had told Drew anything about their date, but part of him wondered if she'd ever told Drew why she watched *Top Gun* so much. Did she ever allow herself to lean on someone?

When the three of them were the only ones in the room, Karissa looked between the two men, but quickly settled on Mick. "You might as well know that the rest of the story going around the school is that Drew's sister got your girlfriend arrested."

Drew scowled and balled his fists before relaxing them. "I don't like my sister being criticized when she was just doing her job."

"So it's true?" Karissa asked, turning to Drew, her mouth open in surprise. "Mick said it wasn't."

"No, I said I didn't have a child or a convict girlfriend," Mick corrected. He eyed the vending machine, but decided he should probably sit and defend his honor. "That wasn't true."

"That's not what you told my sister." Drew picked up his loaf of banana nut bread and paused. For a second Mick thought Drew was done talking, but since Karissa was their only witness, he apparently felt comfortable putting it all out there. "And as far as you taking her on a date, I don't know what game you're playing, but leave Olivia out of it."

Mick ground his teeth and counted to ten. He wasn't going

to defend himself since he didn't answer to Drew, but he was going to set him straight on one thing. "I'm not playing games with Olivia. We went out one time, and we won't be going out again." Mick crumpled the donut wrapper in his hand. "Not that it's any of your business."

"My sister is always my business," Drew said with a frown. "She doesn't belong with someone who only dates for fun."

"Newsflash, Dalton, dates are supposed to be fun." Mick barked out a laugh and shook his head. "It doesn't surprise me you don't know that. You wouldn't know what fun is, if I spelled it for you."

Drew was holding the bread in a stranglehold, as if he wished it were Mick's neck. Karissa was silently staring at him, but Mick was beyond caring. Let the two of them think what they wanted. Even if he tried to see Olivia again, it was unlikely she'd agree to it. She'd nearly sprinted away from the hot springs as if she were late for court, and hadn't looked back.

"Just stay away from my sister. She doesn't deserve someone like you," Drew finally said, his voice strained.

Mick met Drew's gaze, his words reverberating through him. He was right. Olivia deserved better. But her brother was still an obnoxious jerk. There weren't enough donuts in the world to deal with Drew Dalton. Mick tossed the wadded trash into the garbage can. "Olivia doesn't need you to look out for her. She does just fine on her own."

"I don't need you to tell me anything about my sister." Drew had reached his limit. He pushed back his chair to stand and walked around the table until he was nearly nose-to-nose with Mick. "You don't know the first thing about her."

But that's where Drew was wrong. Mick had seen firsthand

that Olivia knew exactly what she wanted, had a great sense of humor, and hid her vulnerabilities as well as he did. She was definitely more than a pretty face to him, but what exactly was she? *Someone who doesn't fit in my life. Someone who deserves more.* He'd had dozens of first dates that never went anywhere. Olivia was just another one. No, he knew he was lying to himself with that thought. She wasn't like any woman he'd ever met.

Drew snorted at Mick's silence and left the lounge. Karissa put her hand on Mick's shoulder and patted it. "Don't worry about Drew. You know how he gets about his family."

He nodded and mechanically pushed his chair in so the table looked neat and tidy. Why had he come into the faculty room after school instead of just going home? The donuts hadn't been worth it. At least it was time for his visit with Will. He'd take his mind off of Olivia, and that was exactly what he needed.

His rental wasn't as fast as his Mustang, but he still made it to the farmhouse in record time. He ran his clammy hands down his pant legs, trying to calm his nerves. He was anxious to visit Will. The two weeks since he'd seen him had seemed like an eternity, but Mick knew Will needed to have a chance to bond with his foster family. As he parked and got out, he could hear children laughing around back. As he headed up the stairs to the porch, Wendy met him at the door.

"He's in the backyard. You're welcome to go find him." She wasn't wearing any makeup and her smile was genuine. Once again Mick noted just how open and friendly her expression was. She truly seemed to love people, and it made him glad Will had been given to her. "He's excited to see you today."

"Glad to hear it." Mick changed direction and went around the side of the house. He found Will kicking a soccer ball with the two other boys he'd seen on his first visit here. He looked out of breath, but happy.

"Hey, can anyone play?" Mick asked as he stood and watched them.

"Mick," Will shouted as he ran toward him. His small body barreled into Mick's, and his arms went around his waist. "You can be on my team."

After a game of two on two, then another of Mick against everyone else, Wendy called to them from the door. "Boys, I've got hot chocolate!"

The boys cheered and headed inside. Mick followed slowly behind, picking up the ball and setting it next to the garage.

"You're welcome to stay, too," Wendy said kindly as the boys squeezed past her into the house, shedding their coats as they went. "It's cold out today."

"Thanks, I think I will." He met her at the door, looking beyond her to the three boys who were deciding the age-old question of how many marshmallows made the perfect cup of hot chocolate. "Will looks happy."

"He's a great kid." She looked up at him, her eyes meeting his. "I know it was hard to wait for a visit, but I'm glad you did. We needed that time to set a routine and get to know each other. But you don't have to worry, he definitely has a serious case of hero worship when it comes to you and was thrilled to hear you were coming today."

"The feeling's mutual." Mick followed her into the kitchen. The room was warm and smelled like chocolate chip cookies. It all seemed too good to be true. But Mick's instincts were usually right on about people, and Wendy hadn't set off any alarms. Maybe Olivia was right, and the foster care system was different now. Or at least better than the one he'd experienced.

Olivia.

She was never far away in his thoughts, no matter what he was doing. He'd gone over every moment of their hike, and each time brought up feelings he didn't want to examine. *Focus on Will.* He walked to the table and sat next to him, while Wendy put four mugs of hot chocolate in front of them.

"It's a little hot still, so you can put some milk in it, or blow on it," Wendy cautioned. She looked up when the doorbell rang. "I'll be right back."

Mick felt a prickle of apprehension sweep across his body, and the hairs on his arms stood up. He half-listened to Will tell him about a soccer game at recess, while trying to hear who was at the door. Craning his neck, he caught a glimpse of a woman in a gray coat. It couldn't be. But that voice was burned in his memory. Olivia was here.

The women were coming down the hall toward the kitchen, and Mick hastily leaned forward to take a sip of his hot chocolate and act nonchalant. The liquid burned his tongue, though, and he sucked in a breath, choking as it went down his throat.

They entered the room, and hearing his coughing fit, Wendy quickly went to the sink to get him a cold drink of water. "Oh, I didn't think it was that hot. I'm so sorry!"

Mick took the water, feeling Olivia's eyes on him. "I'm fine." He felt a flush on his neck. "Olivia." Is that all he could say? Her name? The flush felt hotter.

"Hey." She turned to Will, ignoring Mick. "Just came to check on how my favorite soccer player's doing."

Will beamed up at her, a chocolate chip cookie in one hand. "I'm good. Do you want a cookie?"

"I'd love one." Olivia moved closer to Will and ruffled his hair. Mick tamped down how much it affected him to see how genuinely glad she was to be with Will. "How did you know they're my favorite?"

Wendy put another plate of cookies on the table, then turned to face Olivia. "You'd fit right into this family. I think chocolate chip cookies are my most requested snack. Can I take your coat?"

"Thanks." She handed it to Wendy and sat across the table from Mick and Will. The new plate of cookies consumed Will's attention. All Mick could see was Olivia.

She wore gray pants with a matching blazer and her usual white blouse. Every inch the lawyer. *Probably came straight from work,* Mick thought. But he couldn't help remembering how she'd looked on their hike in her red flannel shirt and jeans right before he'd gotten close enough that he almost kissed her. That was the Olivia he'd wanted to get to know better, the one who wasn't asking him to take chances he just couldn't risk.

Mick tore his gaze away from her and took a cookie so he'd have something to do with his hands. Will kept the conversation going with his nonstop recap of recess and school and how much fun he had with Garrett and Joseph, his new foster brothers. Mick was glad for the distraction because he couldn't think of one thing to say with Olivia at the table.

"Okay, time for homework," Wendy said. The boys groaned, but didn't protest as they took their mugs to the sink. "Thanks for remembering to bring your dishes. That's another star on the chart for you three," she added, rinsing them out.

"Will you come back and visit me again?" Will asked, his attention focused on the direction Garret and Joseph had gone in. He did give Mick and Olivia a quick glance and a smile, though. "Both of you?"

"Sure," Mick agreed. "I need a rematch."

"Same teams," Will said with a mischievous grin. He turned to Olivia. "And I'll draw you a picture next time. So you won't forget me."

"I'd love a picture." Olivia bent down to hug him. "But I'll never forget you. We'll see you in a few days."

Mick got a quick hug from Will as well before he headed down the same hall after his foster brothers. He looked happy. Settled. Mick's heart lightened a little.

"How's he doing?" Olivia turned to Wendy. "Is he as good as he seems?"

"He had a bit of a tough time for the first few days, but Garret and Joseph really helped him." Wendy joined them in the doorway. "He still hoards food in his room, but that's getting better day by day. Sticking to a routine has helped him feel more secure. Any news on his mother?"

Mick leaned forward. He was interested in this answer as well.

"There was a possible sighting in Ogden, but that's all I know. As soon as I have any concrete information, though, I'll give you a call." As if on cue, Olivia's phone buzzed in her pocket, and she took it out. Briefly glancing at it, she declined whoever it was, and looked back at Wendy. "I'm so glad he was placed with you."

"Me, too." She walked a little ways down the hall and got

Olivia's coat. "I'm sorry to cut your visit short. Like I said, routine is really important in the early days."

"No problem. I should have called, but I wanted to drop in and say a quick hello." The women were heading toward the front door, and Mick trailed behind them. He was frustrated by his inability to contribute to the conversation. One of his talents was being able to put others at ease, but it had gone out the window the moment Olivia walked in. Not one comment came to his mind.

She had her coat on and was saying goodbye. He needed to say something before she went outside and got in her car. He moved closer to Olivia and addressed Wendy. "Thanks again for the cookies and cocoa." He intended to leave the same time Olivia did so they could at least walk out together.

He reached for the door at the same time Olivia did, and the moment they touched, a jolt of electricity went up his arm. His mouth went dry, and he couldn't pull his hand away. Olivia didn't move, either, but she boldly met his gaze. Only when she raised one eyebrow at him did he pull back. That magnetizing connection was another thing that made her stand out from every other woman he'd ever dated, but that look on her face told him everything she wasn't saying out loud. The same thing she'd made clear on their hike: What was he willing to do about it? Maybe more than he thought. They needed to have a conversation.

Olivia's lips pressed flat as she stared at him for one more uncomfortable heartbeat. Letting out a little huff of air, she stepped through the door and started down the porch. *Oh no,* Mick thought. *You're not going to walk away without a word again.*

"I owe you an apology," he said as he caught up with her.

"Yes, you do." She didn't even stop, her shoes clicking on the concrete driveway as she strode toward her car. "But probably not for what you think."

"What's that supposed to mean?" He took an extra step and reached for her elbow so she'd have to face him.

She stopped and put one hand on her hip. Meeting his gaze, he was surprised at the level of emotion he saw there—exasperation mixed with attraction. At least he wasn't the only one. "What are you apologizing for?" she asked.

What did she think he needed to apologize for? Was this a test?

Mick shoved a hand into his pocket, deciding to be completely honest. "I shouldn't have left things like I did after our date. It's just . . ." He pushed his other hand through his hair. The words stuck in his throat, but she was impatiently waiting. "I want to get to know you better, but my past is painful, okay? I'd rather leave it behind, and I definitely don't want to dissect it with anyone. You know things about me I'd rather you didn't. I'm sorry."

"I get that. I really do." Olivia tilted her head, her blue eyes pinning him as she took a step toward him. "But is that all you have to say?"

"Yes. No." Her nearness pulled at something inside him, as if an invisible cord was drawing them closer. How could he ever have thought of her as another forgettable first date? He reached out and tugged one of her hands free. Energy zipped between them. "I can't stop thinking about what you said right before you left the hot springs. It touched me. Knowing you battle through similar problems only made the connection I feel for you stronger. And . . . there's definitely something between us I'd like to explore."

The words scared him even as they left his mouth, but they were as bone-deep honest as he could get. If he didn't find out what this thing was between them, he'd regret it for the rest of his life.

"Do you really think you're ready for that?" She reached out with her other hand and he didn't hesitate to take it. "Can you trust me?" She moved closer, her face hopeful and open. She was willing to try. To stay.

In that moment, he wanted more than anything to trust her. To truly believe she wouldn't abandon him like everyone else had. He looked down at her, wanting to touch her hair, but she'd twisted it into a bun, and there were only small wisps that had come loose. He cupped her face with one hand, letting his thumb gently trace her jaw instead, nearly overwhelmed with the desire to kiss her. She watched him, not moving closer, but not drawing away, either. Her words echoed in his head.

When I kiss someone, it means something. Would it mean something if he kissed her now? Would a kiss seal whatever this was between them?

"I trust you," he breathed as he watched her closely for any reactions. He'd never said that before. To anyone. But it felt good to say it—and mean it. His hand moved to the nape of her neck, and he leaned in. She smelled like cotton and snow. He pulled her close and just held her to him in a hug. She fit against his chest and he wanted to keep her there until he'd memorized the moment.

Olivia's phone buzzed again, but she didn't reach for it. Instead, she stretched her arms around his waist.

He stayed still, wanting to savor her nearness a little longer, but the phone kept buzzing. "Are you going to get that?" he asked, nodding in the direction of her pocket.

"No." Her hands slid to his front and rested on his chest. "I'd rather talk about our second date."

"Are you asking me out?" He moved his hands to her shoulders and tilted his head. "Did you get your brother's permission first? Things didn't go well last time he wasn't in the loop."

She shook her head, trying to hide a grin. "Ooh, you're right. I guess we could wait until I talk to Drew first. If you're worried." Unable to hold it in anymore, she let out a laugh and took a half step away, but Mick pulled her back.

"If we wait for your brother's permission, we'll never go out again." He let his hand trail down her arm. "What did you have in mind? What kind of dates do lawyers plan? Should I see if there's a high school debate team tournament nearby or something?"

She bit her lip and looked up, as if seriously considering his suggestion. "Well, that could be fun. Maybe I should check the court schedule to see if there are any interesting trials going on."

He shifted closer to her, letting his hand rest on her waist. "What about watching a TV show about attorneys, and you can tell me everything they're doing wrong?"

She pressed a finger to her chin, but finally made a wry face and shook her head. "Now that sounds fun, but I don't want you to see that side of me yet."

He laughed and bent down, his voice low in her ear. "Well, now that's exactly what I want to do." He heard her breath catch and his pulse started to pound. He turned his head and pressed a kiss to her temple, his lips on her skin making his lungs forget how to do their job. Closing his eyes, he worked to take in a breath and slow his heartbeat. How could that small gesture affect him so much?

She reached up and held her hand to his cheek, as if touching his face grounded her. "I have something else in mind, but it's a surprise. Can you meet me at the high school parking lot tomorrow at seven?" She was breathless as well, her cheeks rosy, eyes bright. She dazzled him, and he didn't want to let her go.

"Can't wait," he managed to say. That little crack of hope she'd opened in his heart on the trail opened a little more as they stood together on the driveway of Will's foster home. And the feeling wasn't as painful as Mick thought it would be.

He still had misgivings and wasn't sure the ugliness could ever truly be banished from inside him, but he knew one thing. He was definitely ready to take the chance Olivia was offering him.

CHAPTER TWELVE

Dusk was starting to fall when Olivia finally pulled into the school parking lot to meet Mick. She'd been in court all day, which was tiring and invigorating all at the same time. Though she was gratified when murder cases progressed, trials also took a lot of mental energy to stay in the game. When it got hard, though, she reminded herself of the date she had to look forward to tonight.

She shifted in her seat and ran a hand through her hair, her thoughts turning to when Mick had said there was something between them he'd like to explore. The look on his face had been tentative, but sincere. Despite the fact that she knew his past, he was willing to take a chance. Her heart turned over in her chest. So was she.

Mick's rental car was in the back of the parking lot, and he was leaning against the driver's side door, his arms folded, waiting for her. He had on jeans with a blue V-neck sweater that fit just right and accentuated his chest and arms. No wonder so many women fell at his feet. Olivia was a little breathless herself.

He smiled when he saw her and straightened. Once she'd parked, he opened the passenger side door and got in. "Hey," he said, pulling his seat belt over his shoulder. "Right on time."

"I have this thing about being punctual. Besides, we have an appointment." She tilted her head, but didn't quite meet his eyes. Hopefully he'd like what she had planned.

"You're being so mysterious. What kind of appointment would an attorney take a date on?" He tapped his finger on his chin. "You didn't sign us up for jury duty, did you?"

"That's your best guess?" Olivia shook her head in mock disappointment. "You're going to have to do better."

"Hmm…" He moved closer. "We're going to a rally to protest lawyer jokes?"

Not many people could keep her laughing during conversations, but Mick was quick on his feet and unpredictable. She glanced over at him, and he grinned, his eyes crinkling adorably. *Irresistible.* "No, but maybe we *should* organize a rally sometime. Have you heard some of those jokes? Lame."

He held up a hand. "Wait, wait, have you heard this one? What do you get when you cross a librarian and a lawyer?"

Olivia groaned. She was pretty sure she'd heard every lawyer joke there was, but hadn't heard this one. "Not you, too. I don't think I want to know."

"You get all the information you need, but you can't understand a word of it." Mick leaned over and nudged her shoulder. "See? Not all lawyer jokes are terrible."

"Yes, they are." She had to admit, seeing this lighter side of him was unexpected, but she liked it. "Just for that, I'm going to let you in on what I have planned." And maybe a little retribution for the lawyer joke. "What if I told you I made us appointments for pedicures?"

Mick pulled back a little, watching her to see if she was serious. Olivia put her best poker face on, concentrating on the road, but keeping him in her peripheral vision.

"Um, that could be fun." He sat back in his seat and faced front. "Sure. Pedicures. I've never done that before."

Olivia could barely hold in a laugh as he tried to hide his grimace. She might as well have asked him to drink spoiled milk. She really shouldn't have teased him like this, but how could she resist after the lawyer joke?

She kept up her story, trying to sound enthusiastic without giving it away. "But this isn't an ordinary pedicure. They have this cool new thing where little fish eat the dead skin off your feet. It sounded adventurous and right up your alley." She glanced at him, the streetlight flickering over his frozen smile.

"Flesh-eating fish? I don't know. That might be a little too adventurous for me." Mick actually shivered, and Olivia grinned.

"Oh, really? Well, I guess we could go do something else." She added an extra dose of disappointment to her voice. "What's something tame and boring that you'd like to do instead?"

He turned toward her with both hands up in surrender. "No, no, if you want to have our feet eaten by fish, then that's what we're going to do. I'm totally up for it."

She gave him her most winning smile and pulled off the freeway, headed for the outskirts of the city. "You trust me that much?"

"I never should have told you about the *Aladdin* thing. You're mocking my pickup line." He was close enough that her heart rate sped up at his nearness. He smelled like fresh laundry with a hint of spiciness. What kind of aftershave was that?

Wanting to take another sniff made it hard to concentrate on driving and keeping the conversation going. Pulling her mind back, she said, "I'm not mocking it; I'm using it." She took another glance at his face. "Is it working?"

He angled himself closer, until his mouth was near her ear. "Maybe. I like that you're trying."

She shivered all the way down to her toes, and her mind went blank. How was he able to reduce her bones to pudding with a few words? Putting her focus on the road in front of her, she took a shaky breath. "H-How was work?"

He chuckled, obviously noting her stutter, but he moved away, putting some space between them. "Work's good. We've moved past the safety tutorials, and now my students are planning out their projects. I've got some creative kids this semester."

At his explanation, Olivia relaxed. Maybe he was like Drew —work was a safe topic he could talk about for hours. "Do they make anything beyond shelves?"

"Beginning classes have set projects, but my seniors have a little more leeway. Some kids stay with the typical cutting boards, tables, stepstools, even treasure chests, but a few branch out. One kid did this incredible carved pirate chest. I wasn't sure he could do a piece that difficult, but he proved me wrong, and it was amazing." His face lit up. It was easy to see that his students were important to him.

Olivia wanted to know more, everything that made up Mick

Donovan. "What's the weirdest thing a student has made?"

Mick leaned back and looked up, thinking for a moment. "I don't know that it was weird, necessarily, but it was definitely creative. It was a bookshelf." He paused when she gave him a sideways glance, but went on. "In the shape of an apostrophe. The project took a lot of work, but looked really good when it was done."

He sounded so proud. Olivia wanted to turn and watch his facial expressions. She always loved driving, but right now she didn't want to have to focus on the road. Yet, the car provided a little bit of intimacy in such an enclosed space, as if they were sharing secrets and no one would hear. "Sounds like you give free rein to creativity in your classroom."

Mick shifted his weight to lean his elbow on the armrest and stretched his legs. "I like watching their faces as they create. To help them see that they can make a block of wood into something beautiful. Woodworking has a lot of life lessons in it, but the best thing about it for me is how calm I feel when I'm creating. I want them to feel that, too."

She changed lanes, wishing they weren't so close to their destination and had more time to talk. She slowed down a little. "How did you get into woodworking?"

Mick turned his face to look out the window as if he wasn't totally comfortable talking about it. "It's a long story, but the short version is, I had an army buddy who loved it, and when we had downtime, he showed me all he knew. Whittling was a stress reliever for both of us."

His voice sounded faraway now, and Olivia wanted to get all the details and draw him near again. Hopefully she'd have another opportunity to ask him more about it. "Maybe I should take up woodcarving, then. I'm always looking for a good stress reliever."

"I'd be happy to show you sometime." He angled in his seat so he could almost face her. "What do you do now for stress relief?"

"Kickboxing. There's nothing like landing a really good kick and hearing the little whoosh go out of the punching bag." She hadn't been to the gym in a while, though. Talking about it made her itch to get back in there.

"Okay, tell me the truth, do you ever imagine someone's face on the punching bag? A defendant? An old boyfriend?"

"All the time. Kickboxing is like free therapy. The best part, though, is getting the endorphins going." Olivia pulled into a warehouse parking lot that had a large sign with a lumberjack on it carrying an axe. She parked in front and turned off the car. "Surprise."

Mick looked over at the sign, then back at her. "I'm no expert on pedicures, but is this place stocked with some sort of exotic creatures that cater to lumberjack footcare?" His confusion was evident, and Olivia laughed again.

"I might have led you a little bit astray after your lawyer joke. This is an axe-throwing range." She grinned as his confusion turned to mock-indignation. "Think you're up for it?"

"More than I am for flesh-eating fish. But I think I need to lodge an objection or something. That lawyer joke was the best one I had." He got out of the car and came around to the driver's side to open her door.

"Overruled," she said as she got out. "I was testing the waters, seeing what your boundaries were. Now I know. You're up for anything."

Mick stayed close to her side, and his warmth stole over her. "Well, I'm up for *almost* everything." He looked at the building as they walked up and held the door for her. "I didn't even know this was here."

"It just opened last month."

They walked in together, and the smell of sawdust hit them immediately. The *thunk* of axes hitting their marks was a regular rhythm as they approached the desk. Over Mick's protestations, Olivia paid the fee, and they went to meet their coach. After a brief tutorial on how to throw axes over the head, without flicking the wrist, they each picked one up.

They stood in the lane, with a wooden target about fifteen feet away, and the coach on a tall stool behind them. "Care to make a friendly wager?" Mick asked, testing the weight of the axe by tossing it from one hand to the other.

"What do you have in mind?" Olivia gripped her axe to get a feel for it.

"First person to get three bullseyes wins. If you lose, you come to my workshop and make something. If I lose, we get fish pedicures together."

"We could do that. Or how about something for tonight? The winner gets to say where we go for dinner." Olivia got into position. "I like bets about food."

"Okay, winner chooses dinner. We'll save my bet for when I win and you ask for a rematch. I'll even sweeten the deal by adding a dessert." Mick followed the coach's instructions and threw, hitting the target just above the bullseye.

"Close." Olivia lined up to take her shot. The axe bounced off the target.

The coach stepped forward from his perch. "Both of those

were good for first tries, but you've got too much spin. You're letting it go just a bit too early. Let's try that again."

Olivia nodded. "Thanks." She walked down the lane to retrieve her axe, then lined up again, pointing the head of it at the bullseye. "I think I've warmed up now."

"Okay." Mick stood next to her, ready to throw his next one. She stepped back and he waited until she was a safe distance away before he threw his axe. *Thwack.* "Bullseye!"

Olivia followed suit, matching his shot by getting her first bullseye. Mick's second one hit below the target. The coach started toward them, starting to give his suggestions, but Mick held up his hand. "Don't worry. I've got this."

They went back and forth for twenty minutes until the final throw, when Olivia got her third bullseye. She pumped her fist in the air. "Yes! I got it! I won!"

Mick put down his axe and wrapped an arm around her shoulders, joining in the celebration. "Hey, you hustled me! There's no way that was your first time throwing axes."

"It's all in the technique. A soft touch. A little spin." She looked up into his eyes, and they locked on hers.

"I thought I *had* a soft touch." He reached out, and his knuckle feathered over her cheekbone. Olivia nearly stopped breathing. The coach and the axe-throwers in nearby lanes faded away, and her focus was only on Mick. He inched closer and for a heartbeat, Olivia thought he would kiss her right there.

"Time's up. I can take your axes for you. Thanks for coming in," their coach said with one more look at his watch. The bubble surrounding Olivia and Mick burst in that nanosecond, and Olivia's thoughts snapped into focus along with the noise and people all around them.

Olivia stepped back, feeling the loss of Mick's warmth immediately. "Thanks for all the help. That was great," she said to the coach who was already taking their axes to the front. She smoothed down her hair before she straightened. *Put your professional face on.* Pulling her mouth into a polite smile, she started to follow him to the desk.

"Yeah, thanks," Mick called out to their rapidly retreating coach. His voice was a little raspy, proving he'd been as affected by what was happening between them as she had.

They headed to the car, and once inside, Olivia pushed the heater on full blast. "So, as the champion, I know a great little Italian place. Out of the way, but amazing food."

Mick did up his seat belt and turned to her. "Sounds great. And as the loser, I'll graciously foot the bill."

She narrowed her eyes and fixed her gaze on him. "You played a fair game, right? This wasn't some grand gesture on your part to let me win so you could pay for dinner?"

"I just got my ego handed to me on the axe-throwing range. From now on, I'm your humble servant." He smiled wide enough to show the dimple in his cheek, and the butterflies in her middle started up again. When he was relaxed, he had a magnetism and boyish charm that captivated her the longer she was with him. All the defenses she'd ever made for charming men were slowly fading away. What was it about this guy?

The restaurant wasn't far, and soon they were being ushered to a table in the back. There were a few other couples there, but with the candlelit atmosphere, it was easy to pretend that she and Mick were the only ones in the room.

Mick leaned close and picked up her hand from the table, interlacing her fingers with his. "I had a great time tonight."

The butterflies going through her middle flapped harder as his palm met hers, and she couldn't stop her lips curling into a smile. "Me, too." She was happy. For the first time in a long time.

Her phone buzzed right before the waiter came to take their order. Olivia thought about ignoring it, but checked the caller ID, just in case. Sam Wood, her boss. All the happiness she'd felt a moment ago turned to a black ball of dread. The district attorney never called her unless it was bad news or an emergency. "Sorry, I've got to take this. It's my boss." She swiped the screen and held it to her ear. "Hello?"

"Hey, sorry to bother you," Sam said, his familiar brusque tone coming over the line. "I thought you'd want to know. The police found Hannah, and it's not good. Officers spotted the stolen car and she bolted. Led them on a high-speed chase and rolled it. She's in critical condition. Can you get over to University hospital right away?"

Olivia looked at Mick, whose expression had turned serious and concerned, all the smiles and laughter gone. "I'll be right there." She ended the call and picked up her purse. "They found Hannah, but she's critical. She might not make it. I've got to get over to the hospital."

Mick took her hand and squeezed it. "I'd like to be there. For both you and Hannah."

For a brief moment, Olivia closed her eyes, relishing the feeling of being able to face a crisis with someone at her side. At least for tonight, she wasn't alone.

It was a feeling she could get used to.

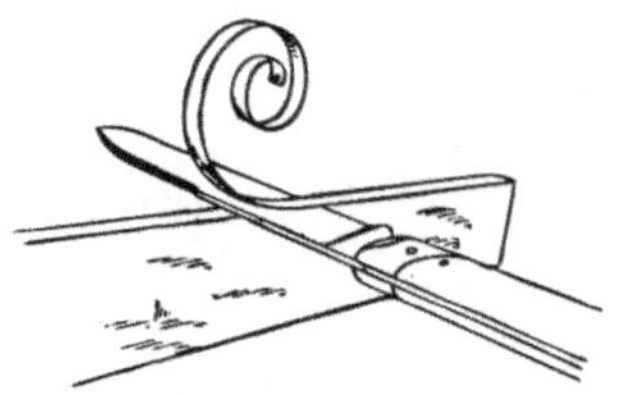

CHAPTER THIRTEEN

As Olivia drove to the hospital, all Mick could think about was Will. If Hannah died, he'd be an orphan at seven. That would be devastating. "Did he say what her injuries were or anything about what happened?"

"Just that she'd been in a car accident fleeing police and was in critical condition." Olivia glanced over at him. "In your car. That's how they spotted her."

Mick frowned and shifted in his seat. The Mustang seemed so trivial now. "I don't care about the car. I care about how this is going to affect Will. No matter what she's done, she's his mother and Will loves her. If she doesn't make it, he'll have lost his only parent." He ran his hand through his hair. "Do you think we ought to tell him? Bring him to the hospital?"

"Let's wait until we know more." Olivia stopped at a red light and leaned toward him. "Are you sure you want to come? It might be a lot of waiting around."

"Yes, I want to be there." He didn't know why. It wasn't as if he were close to Hannah. But he felt like he owed it to Will somehow. "If that's okay with you," he added.

"You know it is. I doubt we'll be allowed to see her, though. Stuck in the waiting room, most likely."

"That's okay. I used to be impatient," he said. "Being a schoolteacher helps with that. Sometimes I can teach the same techniques over and over and then when the student is about to give up, it finally clicks. There's nothing like seeing everything fall into place and they get it."

"Waiting is such a huge part of my job. Waiting for juries, for judges, for warrants. There's always something I'm waiting on, so I had to learn to cope. But vigils are a different story, especially when this outcome is so important for Will." The light turned green, and Olivia focused on driving. "I wonder if she was under the influence."

A flicker of anger went through Mick that quickly flamed into sadness for Hannah. She had a great son, but she hadn't been able to properly care for him while addiction fueled her choices. Now she might have to leave Will behind.

It made him wonder about his own father. Had he given Mick a second thought? Or had his addiction been his only concern? Deep down, Mick knew the answer, and the child he'd been still mourned that truth. The abandonment was hard to put totally behind him sometimes, and it was frustrating to think that Will might have the same difficulties.

About fifteen minutes after the phone call, Olivia was parking in the hospital's lot. She didn't show any anxiety on the outside, but she hurried into the ER, barely looking back to make sure he followed. Mick easily caught up with her and kept pace. He wanted to get an update as soon as possible.

Once inside the ER waiting room, Olivia focused on a man in a rumpled suit, talking on the phone. *That must be the D.A.* Mick vaguely remembered seeing Sam Wood on news conferences, put together and confident. Right now, he looked like he'd put in a long day. His tie was askew, and he had more than a five o'clock shadow on his jaw.

Sam held up a hand, silently asking her to wait while he finished. A minute later, he disconnected the call. Letting out an exhale, he rolled his shoulders before he faced Mick and Olivia. "Thanks for getting here so fast."

"We weren't far away." Olivia motioned toward Mick as she made introductions. "Sam, this is Mick Donovan, the man who helped me locate Hannah and her son a few weeks ago."

Well, that was stretching the facts a bit, but Mick didn't contradict her. "Nice to meet you." The two men shook hands.

"Any updates?" Olivia asked, as the trio sat down in the waiting-room chairs.

"Not really. She's got some serious head injuries, and they'll be taking her to surgery soon. The police and doctors are keeping me informed, and we've got a guard outside her room." Sam pulled on his tie as he spoke, as if he wished he could take it off. The limp strip of material was barely hanging on as it was.

Sam's words sank in and Mick raised his eyes to Sam's face. "Why does she need a guard? Has she run before?"

Sam leaned forward, resting his elbows on his knees, and looked at the floor. "In addition to her injuries from the crash, she had a gunshot wound to her chest. We're not sure what we're dealing with right now."

She'd been shot. Mick's lungs squeezed and he sucked in a breath. "Should we be concerned about Will's safety?" Mick's brow furrowed with worry. Would whoever Hannah was involved with come after her child?

"With her low-man-on-the-totem-pole position in the oper-ation, I don't think they'd hurt her kid. Their job is to make sure she can't give us information." He took out his phone. "I'll notify the Lincoln PD, just to cover our bases. They can do a few drive-bys and keep their eyes open."

"And Susan Shepherd is Will's caseworker. We should prob-ably give her a call, too." Olivia took out her own phone. "Do you need her number?"

Sam shook his head and stood, looking down at his phone screen. "No, I've got it. I'll be right back." He walked toward the hallway, his phone already pressed to his ear.

"I'm worried about Will," Mick said quietly, watching him go.

"Sam is thorough," Olivia assured him, reaching over to lay her palm on his knee. "He'll do everything he can to make sure Will and Hannah are protected."

Mick picked up her hand, wanting that connection with her. It was cold, so he covered it with both his own to warm it up. "Are you nervous?"

"Maybe a little. Or it's just cold in here." She smiled, but it didn't reach her eyes. She'd probably dealt with this sort of thing before. Did she have a hunch as to how this would go? Was that why she was nervous?

"Hospitals can be intense for some people," Mick offered,

trying to put his negative energy to the side and think positive. "Or maybe your boss makes you nervous."

Olivia shifted in her seat, but she left her hand in Mick's. "Sam is a brilliant attorney who works harder than anyone I've ever seen. He inspires me."

"Harder than you?" Mick pressed his side to hers, wanting to share his warmth with her, in case she really was cold. "Impossible."

"No, he really does." She looked over at Sam standing in the hall that led to the rest of the hospital, still on the phone. "He's dedicated. Ever since I've known him, he's been all about doing the very best he can to help those who can't help themselves."

"Sounds like someone else I know." He gently squeezed her fingers. "What happens to Will if the worst happens . . . if Hannah doesn't make it?"

Before she could answer, the waiting room doors opened, and an older couple walked in. The woman was holding a tissue to her face, and she'd obviously been crying. They immediately went to the woman behind the desk.

"I'm looking for Hannah Dahlquist," the man said. "We were told she was brought here."

"Are you family?" she asked kindly, moving to her computer screen.

"We're her parents." The woman straightened and glanced around the room. She met Mick's eyes briefly before she focused back on the nurse. "Please. I need to see her. The officer said it was serious, and we needed to come right away."

The nurse checked her screen once more, then walked around the desk. "Come this way."

Mick watched as they passed. Their coats and shoes looked

expensive, and they both carried themselves well. But Mick knew better than anyone that a drug addiction didn't care if you were rich or poor. They obviously cared about their daughter, though, and he was glad to see that.

"Do you think they know about Will or that he's in foster care?" he asked quietly. Olivia had been watching the older couple as well, her eyes on them until they'd disappeared behind the doors that led to the ER treatment area.

"Susan has been in touch with them. They've tried to get custody of Will before, but her father is going through cancer treatments now, and they don't think they can take care of him." She let out a breath. "They were planning regular visits, though. They do want to be part of his life."

Mick leaned his head back, his worry turning to dread. Was Will close to his grandfather? How would a little boy face so much loss if both his mother and his grandfather died? He couldn't imagine. "Hannah has to pull through."

Sam came back, his face grim and Olivia pulled her hand away and stood. "It doesn't look good. She's barely clinging to life." He sat down next to Mick. "Everything is in place to ensure Will's safety, though."

The news about Hannah hit Mick hard. She was probably dying. Chances were good that she wouldn't make it, and Will didn't even know. "Should we get Will here to say goodbye to her?"

Sam pinched his nose, his shoulders slumped. "They wouldn't let him in even if we did. Her injuries are too severe." He looked defeated. "I wish it were different, believe me."

Olivia frowned and paced for a while, as if working out a problem in her head. When she finally sat down, she turned to Sam. "Have the detectives gotten any leads on the shooting?"

"A few. I should be getting another update in about an hour." He pressed back in his seat. "I hate these chairs. No way to get comfortable in them."

Mick agreed. He stood up to get a drink from the fountain, and the door to the treatment area opened. Hannah's parents were outside of a room, hugging each other tightly. A doctor wearing green scrubs slowly stepped away from them, pushing his glasses back onto his nose. Seeing the man's somber expression, Mick knew in his gut it wouldn't be good news.

The doctor walked directly to Sam who stood to shake his hand. "I informed Ms. Dahlquist's parents that she didn't make it. I'm sorry. We did all we could."

Mick had known it was coming, but his stomach still dropped to his toes as the ramifications of those words washed over him.

Hannah was dead.

He hadn't known her well, but she was still a human being, someone he'd talked to and tried to help. And Will's life would be changed forever.

"Did her parents make it in time to say goodbye?" Olivia asked, moving to stand next to Sam.

"Barely. As you can imagine, they're pretty distraught." The doctor glanced at Olivia before turning back to Sam. "We have some paperwork for you before we can release any of her files."

The doctor didn't wait and headed back the way he'd come. Sam followed. "You might as well go home, Olivia," Sam said over his shoulder. "We'll pick this up again tomorrow. Get some sleep."

Go home and get some sleep. That's exactly what Mick had been told when his father died. The words took him back to that moment, back to the anger, the abandonment, the what ifs. He let his chin fall to his chest and stared at the floor. He'd reconciled what happened with his father, knowing as an adult that his six-year-old self couldn't save him, but what if he could have done something more for Hannah? Should he have stayed with Hannah that night instead of leaving her passed out on the couch? Maybe he should have been more of a friend when she first came to town. It might have made a difference.

"If only I'd intervened sooner," Olivia said with a sigh, echoing his thoughts. "Maybe I could have prevented this."

"I was thinking the same thing about myself." Mick raised his face to look at her. "I know the 'if only' game isn't productive, but it's hard not to play it with an outcome like this."

"I'll have to let Susan know, so she can tell Will." Olivia rubbed a hand across the back of her neck. "I don't think we should wait until tomorrow to tell him, and I think we should both be there for emotional support. Will's going to need all he can get."

Mick nodded in relief. "I agree. Thanks for including me."

"You two have a bond. He's going to need you." She reached out for him.

He took her hand and held on. The darkness of his own childhood was always there on the fringes and the situation with Will was showing him how easy those wounds could open again. But things were different now. Mick had perspective, years of counseling, and the healing he'd already worked hard to achieve on his side. He could help Will navigate the future. With his fierce love for his mother, and his confidence that she was coming back for him, news of her death would be a shock and something he'd need to work through for a long time to come.

If Mick could lessen any of that pain for him, he would. "I'll be there."

CHAPTER FOURTEEN

Olivia kept checking her rearview mirror to make sure Mick was still behind her. When they'd left the hospital, he'd asked her to drive him to the school parking lot so he could pick up his car, but now she wished they'd driven to Will's together and picked up his car later. All the way to the school he'd seemed quiet, which was understandable after Hannah's death, but things didn't seem quite so bleak when they were together. She was dreading telling Will, and would have liked to have Mick with her while she sorted out her feelings on how best to approach it.

Susan had called ahead to let the Jurgens family know what was going on, and said she would meet them at the house. When Olivia pulled up, the porch light was on, giving off a warm, welcoming glow. Susan's car was in the driveway and she was still in the driver's seat. Grateful she'd waited, Olivia parked behind her and got out. Mick did the same.

They walked up the porch steps together, but once at the

top, Susan didn't ring the doorbell right away. Instead, she turned and reached out to shake hands with Olivia, then Mick. A breeze had picked up, and Susan's shoulder-length red hair blew in her face.

She pushed it away with one hand and pulled her puffy black coat closer around her with the other. "Good to meet you both. I wish it were under better circumstances."

Mick nodded, and Olivia wished she dared hold his hand. But this visit felt official, so she held back. "Thanks for coming out tonight," she said, focusing on the caseworker and less on the silent man at her side.

Susan knocked, and Wendy came to the door, ushering them all inside. "Why don't we go into the living room?" She directed them with a tilt of her head. "Will's waiting in there."

Susan went first, followed by Olivia and then Mick. Will was waiting on the couch with a man sitting by his side, who was dressed in sweats and a sweatshirt, with a beard that nearly touched his chest. But he had kind eyes that were concentrated on Will. He looked up when they entered, though, and stood to greet them.

He reached out to shake Mick's hand. "Hi, I'm Eric Jurgens. You must be Mick. I feel like I know you from all the stories Will's told me."

Olivia walked over, and Eric shook her hand as well. Once all the greetings were taken care of, they sat down. The living room was a good size, but with all the adults, it seemed to shrink. The stone fireplace was the centerpiece, with a formal couch opposite. Wendy and Eric sat there with Will between them. It was oversized enough that another adult could have fit, but Olivia noticed Mick didn't try to wedge himself in, though she could tell by the way he kept his eyes on Will that he wanted to be close. He chose the overstuffed armchair by the couch, as close as he could get without actually being next to Will.

Olivia chose a wingback chair near the window, and Susan chose the matching one on the other side, but she scooted hers closer to where Will was sitting. He was looking at everyone nervously, his eyes wide. The longer it took to get everyone situated, the more anxious he became. Pulling his legs up to make himself as small as possible, he pressed his back into the couch and gripped his knees.

Susan noticed his reaction as well and dove in. "Will, we have some news that might be hard for you to hear." She cleared her throat and leaned forward. "So many people love you. Your mom. Your grandparents. Eric and Wendy. Mick and Olivia."

Will fidgeted with his pajama pant leg and didn't meet Susan's eye. "Something's wrong."

Susan started to say something else, but Mick held up his hand. "Would you mind if I told him?" When Susan nodded for him to go ahead, Mick leaned as close to the couch as he could get. "Buddy, your mom had an accident tonight. They took her to the hospital and did everything they could so she could come back for you. She fought really hard, but . . ." He paused and got off his chair to kneel in front of Will, taking his hands. "I'm so sorry, but she passed away."

Tears welled in Will's eyes as he stared at Mick. "You mean she died?"

Mick nodded. He held out his arms, but Will buried his face in Wendy's shirt instead and sobbed. "You're lying. My mom's coming back for me. She always comes back."

It was hard for Olivia to hold back her own tears as everyone in the room listened to a little boy cry for his mother. Wendy held him close, patting his back, and the scene nearly broke Olivia's heart.

After a few minutes, when he'd quieted, he hiccupped and looked at Mick. "Did she ask about me?"

"She was really hurt when she came in, buddy, so she couldn't talk. But I know she would have asked about you if she could. She loved you. That's what she would want you to remember." Mick patted his shoulder, then sat back in his chair. "Like Susan said, you have a lot of other people who love you, too."

"Your grandma and grandpa want to come visit," Susan told him, gently putting forth the idea. "Do you think you'd like that?"

He climbed on Wendy's lap and snuggled in, then nodded at Susan's question. "They were always nice to me. Brought me gummy bears."

Susan smiled. "I'm sure they'll bring you some more. All grandparents know the best candy to buy."

"My mom didn't like gummy bears. She liked chocolate bars," Will said, the tears starting to fall again. "If I was good at the store, we always bought one with six squares for each of us and split it."

Wendy hugged him again, whispering into his hair that it was going to be all right. Even as she heard the words, Olivia knew things would never be the same for Will, but he had a really good chance of getting through this. He had a good support system and a lot of people looking out for him now. They would all help him.

Mick had been quiet through this whole exchange, and when Olivia looked over at him, he had a strange look on his face. He grasped the arms of his chair while watching Wendy and Will together with a laser focus.

What is he thinking?

The mood in the room was heavy, Will's hiccups reminding them at regular intervals of his grief and what was ahead of him as he came to terms with his mother's death.

Susan leaned forward and wiped away her own tears. "I'm so sorry, Will. Do you have any questions for me? Is there anything I can do?" When he shook his head, she turned to Eric and Wendy. "I know it's late. This news will take some time to process."

"Have any arrangements been made yet?" Eric asked softly. "Do we need to do anything or prepare Will to be involved in that?" He put his arms around Wendy and Will, holding them as if he could shield them.

"The grandparents are going to let us know. As soon as I have any details, I'll give you a call." Susan stood up and walked over to the couch where Will was still in Wendy's arms. "I'm really sorry, Will."

He nodded, but didn't say anything. Olivia stood as well, feeling helpless, wanting to reach out to both Will and Mick, but not knowing how.

She crouched down so she could be at Will's level. "I'm sorry, too. If you want to talk about anything at all, you can call me, okay? Wendy has my number."

She could feel Mick's gaze on her, but when she glanced over, he looked away. Her stomach knotted into worry. Would he pull away again?

Mick slowly stood and held his arms out for Will. This time, the little boy rose, and when he came close enough, Mick scooped him up in a tight hug. Tears ran down both of their cheeks as they held each other, and Olivia cried along with them. Two boys who'd lost so much. She brushed away her tears, but they just kept coming. Mick was still affected by the losses he'd suffered, and watching him, his hair tousled, his emotions raw, he looked vulnerable and boyish. Would Will carry his wounds for the rest of his life, too?

They finally released each other, and Mick set him down. He whispered in Will's ear, and the boy nodded before giving him one more hug. Mick tried to wipe his tears with one hand while he squeezed Will's shoulder with the other. He was rewarded with a watery smile before Will went back to Wendy and Eric.

"Thank you for coming," Wendy said. She glanced at Will, and Olivia knew his foster mother didn't want to leave him, even for a moment.

"We can see ourselves out," Olivia assured her, catching her eye as Will got back into her lap. "We'll see you soon."

Olivia fell into step beside Mick as they followed Susan outside, closing the door softly behind them. Susan stopped to zip up her coat, then angled to face Olivia. "I'll let Wendy know the counseling resources available for Will and see if we can't set something up. He may need someone to talk to after what's happened."

"Thanks for being so on top of everything," Olivia said, moving closer and laying a hand on her forearm. "I know you've got a lot on your plate right now."

Susan shook her head and patted Olivia's hand. "Every one

of the kids under my care is my top priority." She let go and started down the steps, leaving Mick and Olivia on the porch. "I know you feel the same about your legal cases. It's a calling, not a job."

They both paused and looked at each other in acknowledgment of the truth in that statement. Susan had nailed what Olivia had never really been able to express. A calling is exactly what her job felt like. Not many people could understand that, but Susan got it.

Olivia waved and watched Susan get into her car, maneuvering in the wide driveway to get around Mick and Olivia's vehicles. Mick stood next to her, but she couldn't read his expression. Wanting to be close and figure out what was going through his head, she turned and reached for him. They stood there for a moment, his hands warm on hers. His touch never failed to make her heart race, but this time an edge of fear accompanied the blood rushing through her. "Do you want to go somewhere and talk?"

He looked at her for a long beat, as if he wanted to say something, but then shook his head, obviously deciding against sharing his thoughts. "I can't."

Her heart sank. Were they back to square one? "Can't or won't?"

Mick ran a hand through his hair. "I just need to sort some things out. Can I call you?"

"Sure." Olivia stepped back, trying to keep her face neutral when everything she thought they'd been building was crashing down around her ears. "Give me a call when you're ready."

She walked down the porch stairs, hoping he would call her name, tell her to come back, but he didn't. She could feel his eyes on her as she got into her car, the air around them silent and heavy. Something was wrong, but she couldn't help him if he wouldn't trust her. After putting the car into reverse, she backed out and drove down the road, making a few turns before she was sure he wouldn't pass by her as he went home. Then she bent over the steering wheel and let the tears come.

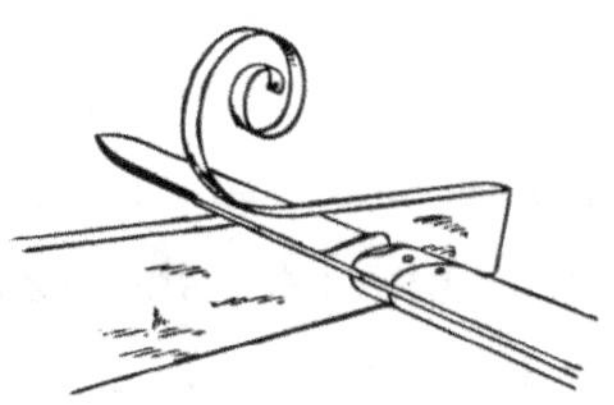

$\mathcal{M}$ick could hardly keep his eyes open and all he wanted to do was lay his head down on the desk. He couldn't wait for his last class to end so he could go home and sleep. At the same time, sleeping ran the risk of his nightmare coming back. Catch-22.

Hearing Will's sobs last night had shaken him, echoing through his mind and combining with his own feelings as a child when he realized he was alone in the world. All his old anxieties had surfaced. He'd driven home as quickly as he could to get out of the darkness, and nearly sprinted into the house to turn on all the lights. When every room was brightly lit, he organized his food pantry, reassuring himself that he had food any time he wanted it. They were old obsessive habits, left over from his childhood, but things that helped him cope. After he'd finished in the pantry he worked on the owl feathers, the rhythm of carving offering some comfort, but he couldn't center himself, so he'd gone for a run. But now his body was telling him in no uncertain terms that he needed to rest. Soon.

He hadn't known how to share his feelings with Olivia last night, though she'd given him the chance. And he'd hurt her. They'd connected on a different level yesterday, first at the axe-throwing range and then at the hospital, but all the exhilaration of that closeness had turned murky after the news of Hannah's death. He could only imagine how confused she felt.

"Mr. Donovan, I need you to approve my design." The student looked warily at him as if she was afraid he'd bark at her. He was usually a laid-back teacher, but today he couldn't get comfortable in his own skin. He'd hurt Olivia. He was hurting for Will. And there wasn't a way to fix either of those situations at the moment. The least he could do was not be curt with his students.

"That looks great, Allie," he said. "I like how you put the little extra curlicue into the shelf base." She really did have a talent with wood. He knew woodworking wouldn't be a career for many of these kids, but at least they'd tried their hand at a creative outlet. Shaping a block of wood had always soothed him. In his darkest days, he'd used carving to speak peace to his soul. But that hadn't been enough today.

Mercifully the bell rang, and the kids packed up, chatting and talking to each other, but only giving him uncertain glances. He normally joked and chatted with them and made sure the shop was meticulously clean before he went home, but today the need to leave was almost overwhelming, so he just gave everything a once-over.

He locked his classroom and headed for the parking lot, keeping his head down. High school halls were like running a gauntlet and he zigzagged through kids milling around lockers. Finally making it outside, he took a deep breath and looked up, hoping for light, but the gray sky was unyielding, refusing to let any sunshine through. With a resigned sigh, he walked to his car and pulled his keys out. Once he'd unlocked it and got in, he sat and watched more students leave. Were they going home to a safe environment? And if not, would they tell anyone? He pressed his fingers to his temples.

Don't go there.

He always watched for signs in his students that they might need help, and he reminded himself that he hadn't seen any. The kids knew they could trust him, and that was all he could do. Obsessing over it wouldn't help anyone.

After five minutes of breathing exercises, he drove out of the parking lot and headed home. But as he passed Rosie's, he noticed Taunya's car in the parking lot. He hadn't been to the restaurant since Olivia had questioned him.

Did Taunya know about Hannah's death? He did a U-turn and drove into Rosie's parking lot. Trying to sleep was a gamble since he might lie there and stare at the ceiling. Getting something to eat and talking to a friend seemed like a better option.

He found a space and got out, glad there weren't many people here yet. Students usually gathered after school for Rosie's famous scones and jam, and then the crowd filled to capacity around dinnertime. But right now, there were only a few cars here, so there might be a chance for peace and quiet and a little conversation.

He went inside, and Taunya saw him come in. She smiled and grabbed a menu. "It's been a while," she said in greeting. "What's been going on with you?"

He cleared his throat. "Hey, do you have a break coming up? I'd like to talk to you about something," he said, as he followed her to a table in the back. Telling her about Hannah wouldn't be easy. He had too many emotions of his own attached to the situation.

"I can take a break right now." She handed him the menu. "Let me go tell Emma to cover for me. I'll be right back."

Mick sat down and opened the menu. He didn't need to look at it, since he practically had it memorized, but the thought of telling Taunya made him jittery so he flipped the pages. He closed it again, just as Taunya slipped into the seat across from him. "What's going on?"

He ran his hands over his face before he clenched them together on the table. "Do you remember Adrienne? Whose real name was Hannah, and how she stole my car?"

"Yeah." Taunya tilted her head far enough to one side that her ponytail touched her shoulder. Her eyebrows pulled down in concentration, obviously trying to understand where he was going with this. "Is everything okay? Did you get your car back?"

"No." He took a breath. Taunya had tried to help Hannah, too, had worked with her, knew her. But she obviously didn't know what had happened. This was the moment of truth.

Just say it. He swallowed, his mouth suddenly dry. "Hannah was in a car accident last night. She didn't make it."

Taunya leaned back and put her hand over her mouth. "Oh no! What about her son?"

"He's in a foster home. A really good placement, actually. Lots of support." Mick thought about Will in Wendy's arms and knew he was speaking the truth. That was the only bright spot in this whole mess—Will had found a home.

Taunya reached out and took his hand. "I heard you were close to her kid. That's got to be hard."

Mick looked down at their hands. Hers were warm and for a split second, he wished they belonged to a lady whose fingers were perpetually cold.

She patted his hand and drew away. "Is there something else? I heard you had some trouble with that lawyer lady," she said.

Rumors had followed him around for years, and they'd never bothered him before. But now, the ones involving him and Olivia were getting under his skin. "Do I want to know what the gossip mill is saying?" He'd certainly given everyone something to talk about lately.

"I've never seen you so fidgety before and you look like death warmed over. Have you slept at all? What's really going on?" She rested her elbows on the table, watching him carefully. "And you know you can trust me to keep anything you say in confidence."

That was true. Taunya wouldn't ever say anything bad about anyone. She was one of the nicest people he'd ever dated. "It's complicated," he finally said.

"Relationships always are. Is she suing you or something?" Taunya lifted her palm and rested her cheek on it. "She looked pretty intense when she was calling the cops on Adrienne. Or Hannah. I don't think I'll ever be able to call her anything except Adrienne."

"She's not suing me." He looked away, trying to figure out how to explain what was going on with him and Olivia in a way that would make sense to someone else. "It might be easier if she were, actually. That would be more straightforward."

"You asked her out, didn't you?" Taunya caught his eye and when he nodded, she groaned. "Oh, Mick. You never could resist a challenge. I'm guessing it didn't go well."

"Well, the first date didn't. But the second one did." He sat back, remembering the fun they'd had axe-throwing and how badly he'd wanted to kiss her. "I don't know. When I'm with her, I feel like I can be myself. At the same time, there are parts of me that I don't want anyone to see, but I can't hide them from her. Last night, I . . . she wanted to talk and I turned her away. She was hurt. Probably thinks I don't trust her."

The sad part was that he did, but couldn't seem to figure out how to share what he was feeling. No one had ever gotten close enough to ask.

"And?" She waited for him to continue. When he didn't, she prodded him on. "What are you going to do about it?"

He fiddled with the edge of the menu and couldn't meet her gaze. "I know I need to talk to her, but it scares me." Finally lifting his face, he looked at his friend.

She wasn't staring at him in pity, but her brow furrowed as if deep in thought. "Are you in love with her?"

The question took him aback, but he immediately dismissed it. "You know me, I don't fall in love."

"I know the *old* you. The guy sitting in front of me is someone new. Someone who *could* fall in love." Taunya smiled. "I didn't think I'd ever see that happen, actually, and it makes me happy that I have."

Mick tugged at his shirt collar, trying to loosen his tie a bit. "Whoa, whoa, don't go jumping to conclusions. I haven't known her very long." But he cared about her. She was the first woman in a very long time that he'd truly been afraid of losing.

Taunya waved her hand airily. "That doesn't matter. When the heart knows, it knows, even when you can't admit it yet. But be honest, is there a chance you could love her?"

He thought of Olivia's laugh when she'd beat him at axe-throwing, of her tears at Will's loss last night. "Yeah, I think I could." The words sank into his soul, chasing away some of the darkness there. He'd made a vow never to let anyone else into his life, to never give anyone the power to hurt him, but Olivia had slipped past all his defenses.

"I think you've already fallen in love with her, but you're fighting it." Taunya leaned over the table with a grin. "Have you kissed her?"

Mick rolled his eyes. "I'm not going to answer that."

Taunya's eyes twinkled with mirth. "Well, if I know you, you've at least thought about it. But even I can see this thing with her is more than your normal flirtation." She gave a dramatic sigh. "And my track record continues. Every guy that dates me falls in love with the girl he dates right *after* me. It's a curse."

This time Mick was the one who reached for her hand. "You're so amazing. The right guy will come along and snatch you up in a heartbeat. I don't doubt that for a minute."

She smiled and squeezed his fingers. "Well, he better hurry up. I'm tired of kissing all the frogs and not getting my prince." She looked in the direction of the kitchen, where Emma was waving at her. "I guess my break time is over."

"Thanks for the chat. I needed a friend today." He handed

her the menu, and though she took it from him, she didn't move away.

"What you really need is to go talk to your lady lawyer. Tell her what you just told me. See what happens." Taunya turned to go to the kitchen, but said over her shoulder. "Maybe she'll surprise you."

Mick had no doubt that Olivia would surprise him. But he didn't want it to be the kind of surprise that would break his heart. Was Taunya right? Was he falling in love with Olivia, but couldn't admit it? And if Olivia cared about him at all, had she given up on him after last night?

He got up from the table. Food didn't sound appealing anymore. He needed to find Olivia. Even if he didn't have a define-the-relationship talk with her, he didn't like the way they'd left things last night. He was going to tell her that, and confide what was going on with him.

And what better time than right now?

CHAPTER SIXTEEN

The deli was crowded today and Olivia considered taking her sandwich back to her office. She needed a change of scenery more than she needed peace and quiet, though, so she stayed. The young man who'd known what her "usual" was came by to wipe down tables and smiled at her.

"You should get some stock in the company or something with as much as you come in." He bent down to wipe the table next to hers. "Maybe they'd give you a discount."

She chuckled. "Aren't you afraid I'd end up being your boss?"

"Hey, I know what sandwich the boss likes, so I might have an in for promotions." He winked. "Am I right?"

"Maybe I'll look into sandwich shop stock." The truth was, sometimes this little deli was her sanity-saver, a short escape from the office where she could eat and gain a little perspective. But it wasn't working today.

The bell above the door jangled, and David squeezed into

the shop, trying to fit around the customers standing in line. Olivia groaned. He was the last person she wanted to see today. She wiped her mouth on a napkin and watched him weave through the crowd to her table. "How did you know where to find me?"

"The receptionist told me you eat here sometimes." He gave her a once-over, and his eyes lit with appreciation. "I love that outfit. I'd love it even more if it were red. Maybe with a little higher heel to show off your amazing legs."

Olivia looked down at her black suit jacket and matching pants. The image of her going before a judge in a red suit and stilettos nearly made her laugh out loud. "I'll pass that on to my personal shopper," she said, mildly. "I was just finishing up."

He turned the chair across from her around and straddled it. "May I join you?" he asked belatedly, since he'd already sat down.

"Like I said, I'm getting ready to leave." She was going to have a talk with Emily. Receptionists weren't supposed to give out personal information. Were lunch locations considered personal? She'd have to think of her arguments in favor of that later.

David gave her his most charming smile and rested his chin on his palm. "I've been thinking about what you said in your office. And I think I've come up with some arguments about why I deserve a second chance. Once I've made my case, then whatever answer you give me, I'll take that as final."

Olivia sighed. Anything to get this over with once and for all. "Do I have your word on that?"

"Yes." He took a breath and let it out. Holding up a finger, he said, "Okay, first of all, I've learned my lesson. You don't like it when I flirt with other women when I'm with you, so I won't do that."

"It's not just me. Any self-respecting woman wouldn't put up with that," Olivia pointed out. "And also, how would you prove that you've learned that lesson?"

"You'd have to trust me." He pulled his mouth into a grin. "Which would solve a lot of problems between us."

"I'm not willing to do that. Once you've lost my trust, it's hard to earn back." She crossed her legs and interlocked her fingers around her knee. Did he really believe a word of what he was saying?

Undeterred by her lack of trust, he held up a second finger. "I know what I want in life and won't settle." He stared at her intently, which only served to remind her of a witness who was lying and trying to hide it. "You and I are magic together. We're both beautiful people with great jobs. It would be a crime against the universe not to try again. You wouldn't want to risk the wrath of the universe, would you?"

Olivia was pretty sure the universe hated her at the moment, no matter what happened with David. "Is there anything else?"

"I rest my case."

Olivia stared at him. That was it? That was his argument for a second chance? She repeated his words to make sure she understood his last point. "We're beautiful people with great jobs. But I'm an assistant D.A., and you're an architect."

"Exactly. I design functional, yet breathtaking spaces, and you put bad guys in prison." He pushed his hair away from his forehead, the movement so smooth she wondered if he practiced it in front of a mirror. "And we both look good doing it."

Pushing away the image of him in front of a mirror practicing running his hands through his hair, she focused on their conversation. "So, your arguments are that you've learned your lesson about flirting, and that we look good together. Do I have that right?"

He leaned forward, his eyes wide, and he reached for her hands. "Do you need another reason? Would it make a difference if I said I love you?"

"That's a pretty big step for hardly knowing each other." She drew her hands away and folded them in her lap. "David, all of the evidence points to you only wanting the women you can't have. You see me as some sort of challenge, but you shouldn't. That ship has sailed."

"It can come back into port. That's why I'm here."

Olivia realized she was tapping her foot on the floor and forcibly stopped herself. It was no use being frustrated with him. "Let me see if I can say this another way. What's my favorite movie?"

He sat up straighter and leaned both arms across the table, his ever-present smile still in full force. "We haven't had any movie dates yet, but if you tell me yours, I'll tell you mine." Olivia cringed at his flirty voice. Did he really think that would help him at this point?

The bell on the door jangled again. Grateful for any interruption, she turned to look. Her mouth nearly dropped open when a familiar figure stepped through, a little windblown and in the clothes he must have worn to teach school today. He cleaned up nice in khakis and button-down shirts.

Mick scanned the deli, and the moment he spotted her, he headed over. The fluttery feelings in her middle started again, but she tamped them down. He hadn't wanted to talk last night, and she'd known he was pulling away from her emotionally.

Was he here to tell her he was done exploring what they had? That it was over? She clenched her jaw. Whatever it was he had to say, she'd be polite and go back to the office with all the dignity she could muster.

Mick made it to the table and looked at David, then her. "The receptionist said I might find you here. She didn't mention you were with someone. Would it be better if I came back later?"

Olivia gritted her teeth. She was definitely going to have a talk with Emily. *Please don't let him break up with me in the middle of the sandwich shop.*

"No, it's fine. David was just leaving."

David ignored Mick and kept his eyes on Olivia. He jabbed a thumb in Mick's direction. "Is he the reason you won't give me a second chance? Or is he a client?"

In a way, she suddenly realized, Mick *was* the reason she hadn't thought twice about David. Mick had shown her that there were still good men in the world who cared more about their fellow man than their image. Although it wasn't that long ago that she'd believed Mick was a player, he'd shown her his real self, and that's the man she was sorry to lose.

"No, he's not a client. And the reason I won't give you a second chance is because we aren't compatible. In any way." She emphasized the last three words so he wouldn't bring up her looks, outfit, or job in front jof Mick.

David glanced sideways at Mick and raised his eyebrows. "Is she always this stubborn?"

Mick took that as an invitation to sit down. Olivia considered standing up and asking him to come to her office so they could speak in private. At the same time, maybe it was best to get the whole thing over with, so she stayed where she was.

"She's always seemed a little on the stubborn side to me," Mick agreed, mildly.

"You're one to talk." Olivia pressed her lips together. He didn't seem upset or angry, but she knew he'd broken things off with dozens of women. Maybe he was comfortable with this part of the dating game.

"How do you know Olivia?" David leaned his arm on the table again as if he'd met up with an old friend and was settling in for a chat. She moved her sandwich out of the way, her table space getting smaller and smaller. Deciding she'd never be able to eat now, she wrapped up her leftovers. If only she could wrap up this conversation as quickly.

"We have a mutual affection for knives and axes. She's got a wicked throw," Mick said with a straight face. "I'm a wood shop teacher," he added. "Lots of knives, saws, and spinning blades. I was glad to find out we had something in common."

Olivia frowned, but a little part of her was happy he had fond memories of their date, too. But why would he bring that up?

David glanced at her with wide eyes. "You have a mutual affection for knives? Do you know how dangerous that is?" He frowned and sucked in a breath, which made his nostrils flare. He looked like a professor about to deliver a lecture to a delinquent student. "What if you cut yourself? Not only would you mar your perfect body with a scar, but you could have a serious accident. How would you explain your carelessness to a judge? You could ruin your reputation over a silly hobby."

She'd never been good with lectures. Or being told what to do. "Hobbies aren't silly. They're relaxing. Having a knife spin just the right way, hitting the target right on the money. There's no other feeling like it." She leaned in, and gestured for David to come closer. He eagerly complied. "And just for your information, my perfect body already has a few scars. I was a tomboy as a kid."

David's eyes lit up again as he tilted his head to give her another once-over. "Mmm . . . I've never seen any."

Olivia restrained herself from rolling her eyes. "Sorry. I'm not in a scar-showing mood today. But I'm pretty sure my knife-throwing hobby is safe. For me, anyway."

"I don't know about that." Now it was Mick's turn to pull them all in, as if he was about to tell another secret. "I didn't want to say anything, but I think this is almost an addiction with her. Like, she has aichmomania or something."

The confused look on David's face was so comical, Olivia could hardly hold back her laughter. She glanced away and played with the edge of the plastic covering her sandwich to keep her face impassive. "Mick," she said softly. "You weren't supposed to tell."

David had already pulled out his phone. "How do you spell that?"

Mick politely told him and when David finally found the definition, he shook his head and said in disbelief. "She's addicted to *sharp objects?*"

Keeping his eyes on David, Mick shrugged. "I'm not a professional or anything, but we were out one night, and she wouldn't let me leave until she'd shown me how many times she could hit a tiny target. With an *axe*. It was scary how into it she was. And how accurate she can throw."

"Does she carry sharp objects with her? I wouldn't think she could, what with all the security they have at her office and the courthouse." David looked down at her purse. "Something like that might cut through the lining and hurt someone." He moved away slightly as if he expected the blade to pop through the side of her purse right then.

"I'm sitting right here, you know. You can ask me if I have any knives or other sharp objects on me." She reached for her purse sitting on the floor next to her feet. "And the answer is, of course I do. Maybe I should show you my favorite. It's German steel with a drop-point blade." She pulled at the zipper on the outside of her purse, as if she were going to open it. Would David call her bluff?

He looked horrified at her revelation. He held up his hands. "No, no, that's okay. I get the point." He swallowed and stood up. "Well, you know what I mean. It's not that I mind that you have a hobby, it's just that I'm not into anything extreme."

She touched his arm. "You never know until you try. Maybe you should come to this axe-throwing place I know. Try it out. Just once."

He pulled his arm back. "That's okay. My hands are my livelihood. Who would draw the plans if I were out of commission? No, I wouldn't do anything to jeopardize that." He carefully turned the chair around, making sure not to bump Olivia as if she was just waiting for a reason to pull her knife out. "I'm sorry, Olivia, but this news is too much for me. I don't think it would work between us. With that sort of dangerous addict—I mean, hobby, I wouldn't want to have to worry about you hurting yourself. Or someone else."

"I understand." Olivia managed to hold in a giggle that was close to being uncontrollable. "I guess this is goodbye, then."

David nodded and turned to leave. Before he made it to the door, however, he stopped to talk to a woman standing in line. She was young and blonde, and already laughing at whatever line he'd given her. Olivia shook her head. Once a player, always a player.

Mick followed her gaze, and they both watched David and the woman leave together. She hadn't even placed her order, just followed him out. When the door shut behind them, Mick finally turned to her, his lips pressed tightly together. But when she met his eyes, they were dancing with mirth.

"Do I need to apologize for the aichmomania thing?" he managed to get out.

"Not at all." She put a hand over her mouth, trying to hold her laughter in. A snort escaped, though, and that set off a chain reaction. They both laughed until the tears rolled down her cheeks. Olivia grabbed some napkins to wipe her face. "It was genius," she gasped.

He tipped his head in acknowledgment, his smile wide enough to show his dimple. "I guess knife trivia comes in handy once in a while. Who was that guy? An old boyfriend?"

"I only went on a date and a half with him, but he's been coming around ever since." Olivia crumpled up her napkin, hoping her mascara hadn't run all over. She hardly wore makeup, but put on just enough mascara so it would look like she had eyelashes.

"A date and a half? What happened?" He put his elbow on the table and leaned in.

"Over dinner, he enjoyed looking at and talking to any woman that came across our path. I'd had enough, so I left." She pushed the crumpled napkin next to her empty drink cup. "Not that it matters."

"It matters. I know a player when I see one." His blue eyes were intent, as if she were the only woman in the crowded deli. "I'd hate to see you with a guy like that."

Warmth trickled through her at his words, but she tried not to react. "Everyone in Lincoln says you're a player. Doesn't that bother you?" She truly wanted to know the answer. She'd believed the rumors. If it hadn't been for the situation with Will, she wouldn't have known any different.

"It bothered me at first, but there's a benefit to it. If everyone knows I won't get serious with a woman, there aren't any expectations." Scooting his chair closer, he shifted in his seat as if he couldn't get comfortable.

He bent his head, and the sunlight shone on his face. He hadn't shaved and his hair was mussed enough to know he'd run his hands through it a few times today. Looking closer, she could see the dark smudges under his eyes. Had he slept? What was wrong?

Hoping he hadn't noticed she was staring, Olivia glanced down at the table. "I guess I hadn't thought about it like that." Was he trying to tell her something? That she'd had too many expectations?

He cleared his throat and dipped his head until she looked at him again. "That was good enough before, but you and Will changed things for me. A lot of things."

It took a second for her brain to catch up to what her ears had heard. "What do you mean?" Hope flared in her chest, but she didn't want to get ahead of herself.

He tentatively reached out and took her hand. "I hate the way I left things yesterday. I'm sorry." His touch sent a tremor of warmth up her arm and made her want to draw closer, like a moth to flame.

"I know telling Will was hard, but it seemed like there was something else going on with you."

He blew out a breath, idly stroking her fingers. Her heart beat faster as she waited for him to speak, her focus on the man in front of her, fighting his demons, but still reaching out.

"I shouldn't have walked away," he said finally, raising his chin. "I'm just not used to having someone there for me. I was sort of losing it last night. I had to go home and turn on all the lights and double-check that I had food to eat anytime I wanted it."

His breaths were coming faster and Olivia could see how hard this was for him. She wanted to take him somewhere private, but at the same time, didn't want to interrupt. "Do those things help more than talking to someone?"

He was quiet for a moment, as if weighing his words. "The truth is, when you offered to talk, it was so out of my realm of experience, I didn't know how to handle it."

She interlocked her fingers with his, combining their warmth, wanting him to feel her support. "All I could think was that you were pulling away. That I'd lost your trust."

"It's so hard to explain." He swallowed hard. "Seeing Will's reaction to being orphaned brought back all my old feelings of abandonment. Knowing that my parents weren't ever coming back, that my dad didn't love me as much as his addiction. I thought I'd be alone for the rest of my life because if your own parent can't love you, can anyone else? It was a little over-whelming." He clenched his jaw before he relaxed. Lifting her hand, he kissed the back of it. "I wish I'd told you yesterday. Trusted you more."

"You are now." She gently touched his cheek, wanting to pull him close and comfort him. This strong, beautiful man in front of her had thought he was unlovable. The injustice washed over her, and she wanted to make it right for him. All she could do, though, was tuck this moment of hope close to her heart and cherish it.

His eyes strayed to her lips, and her heart stuttered. She wanted him to kiss her and thought about taking him back to her office. But that didn't seem right, either. Suddenly the table was too big, her chair too far away from his. As if her body had a mind of its own, she drifted closer to him. The fact that they were in public didn't matter anymore.

He watched her, indecision in his eyes. People were all around, jostling each other as they scrambled for open tables. No one was paying attention to what was going on with them, but Mick pulled away anyway, and settled further into his chair, putting a tiny bit of distance between them. Disappointment trickled over her, but it helped that Mick couldn't hide the still-warm intensity in his eyes that revealed his own wish to be alone, too.

Trying to calm her pounding heart, she mirrored his move-ments and sat back. He gave her a lopsided grin and glanced at the door. "I know you've already had to hear one plea for forgiveness today. Can you bear to hear another? Should I beg for a second chance?"

She tapped her finger on her chin. "I guess I can forgive you, since I probably owe you for the whole 'knife addiction.' David couldn't get away fast enough."

"That was the best part." He draped his arm across the back of her chair, and she breathed in his scent of freshly carved wood mixed with his aftershave. It was a heady combination that made it hard to concentrate on anything but him. "Are you free tonight?"

Her heart picked up its pace again. "Do you want to go axe-throwing?" she teased. "Let me show you how it's done one more time?"

"I'm trying not to feed your addiction." He cleared his throat and met her eyes, unsure, but hopeful. "Actually, I'd like to show you my woodshop."

"I'd love to see it." All the strain of the day seemed to melt away. Mick was reaching out, and she was going to meet him halfway.

CHAPTER SEVENTEEN

Mick tapped his fingers on the steering wheel. The fatigue from earlier had been replaced by a nervous energy. He was going to show Olivia his shop. What if she thought it was amateurish or boring? Trying not to show his jitters to the woman sitting beside him was proving impossible. She had this sixth sense that didn't allow him to hide anything from her. It was strange, disconcerting, and comforting all at once.

He drove up to the house and parked in the garage, but didn't immediately get out. Should he tell her what he was feeling? Had she guessed?

Olivia turned in her seat to look at him. "Did you change your mind?" she asked quietly.

He blew out his cheeks. "No. It's just that when I'm upset, I go in there and carve and chisel. There's a little piece of me in every project." He looked at her with a weak smile. "I guess I'm worried that since you know my background, you'll be able to see something that no one else has. See *me*."

She reached out and touched his shoulder. "Would that be so bad? If it's too much, I can wait until you're ready."

Why wasn't he ready now? He couldn't think of a valid reason. And he'd never been nervous to show his work to anyone before. After last night, though, his emotions were raw. He wanted to let her in, but this first step was harder than he'd imagined. Her opinion meant so much to him. *Just do it.* "No, we don't need to wait. I just need to get over myself. I'm not usually this dramatic, promise."

"Says the man who announced that I have aichmomania." Olivia laughed, her eyes sparkling. She was so beautiful when she let herself laugh. Free. Joyful. "I won't forget the look on David's face."

"'What if you hurt yourself and got a scar?'" Mick shook his head at how shallow David had been. "That guy was a piece of work."

"Can I see some of *your* work?" Olivia sobered, nodding toward his house. "I'd really like to."

Mick nodded and took the keys out of the ignition, then came around to open the door for her. He knew how to deal with students who didn't think they'd enjoy woodworking, but came around once they'd seen their own creations. If Olivia didn't show an interest right away, he could still let her see how woodworking was a source of satisfaction. The thought comforted him.

He helped her out of the car and kept her hand in his as they walked around back to the shop. The closer they got, the more centered he became. This was right.

He turned the lock in the door and stepped inside, flipping on lights as he went. He tried to see the shop through her eyes. The totem pole. The rocking chair. The owl. The table and bench, one of the first projects he'd ever made. He peeked at her face, but she didn't stand still. She was moving toward the center of the room.

Stroking the carvings on the back of the rocking chair, she lifted her eyes to meet his. "This is amazing. All of it." She gave each piece a thorough study. "You're an artist. I can't even begin to describe how beautiful your work is."

All of his concerns melted away at her praise. "Would you like to make something?" He motioned her over to the table, excited to draw her into his world. "I'd love to show you how."

"What could I make?" She looked around at his work area, awe in her eyes at the finished projects. "It all looks so complicated. I couldn't ever do anything like what you do."

"You could go with something easy like a shelf or a step stool. Maybe a desk organizer." He started to set out a block of wood and some of his tools. Her choice would tell him a lot about her. With her logical mindset, she'd probably choose the desk organizer.

"Can I carve something? Not anything like your totem pole, but something small, for a beginner." She looked down at all the tools near his workbench, from small carving knives all the way to his table saw.

"Definitely." He thought for sure she'd go for something useful, but she'd chosen to carve freehand. Unexpected and intriguing. He handed her a carving glove and watched while she put it on, then he gave her his best carving knife. "A lot smaller than the axe, but it could be deadly, I suppose," Mick said with a grin. "Sometimes I just take a block of wood, start carving, and see what takes shape. Or, you can use a pattern if you like."

"I'll try seeing what takes shape." She took the block of wood from him. "So I just start carving?"

"Well, sort of. Let me show you." Mick moved behind her and slipped his arms around her shoulders to guide her hands. She shivered, and he anchored her against him. He'd wanted to hold her since he'd seen her at that table in the sandwich shop, and even though he was using a carving lesson as an excuse, it had been worth the wait.

He guided the knife in her hand to the block of wood. "Always carve away from the body, like this." He showed her how to go with the grain. "And make cuts like this."

She leaned back and relaxed. Her clean cotton and sunshine scent washed over him again. His pulse started to pound, and with as close as they were, she could probably feel it. It wouldn't be hard to turn her in his arms and kiss her. What was he waiting for?

He'd been quiet and still for too long and Olivia twisted to see his face. "Could you show me that again?" she asked, her voice low and suggestive.

It was a heady feeling holding her this way. He moved to show her the carving technique again, thankful he'd done it a million times and could do it in his sleep. All he could see was her, feel her warmth against him, want her with him always. Her breathing was as erratic as his, and she leaned to the side, exposing her neck. Mick didn't need a second invitation, and pushed her hair aside to kiss her nape. She slowly took off the carving glove.

"Olivia," he murmured, his lips making a trail up to her ear as she let out a soft sigh. "I've wanted to kiss you for so long." She dropped the knife on the table and turned in his arms as he pressed against her.

Her hands traveled up his chest before linking them behind his neck to bring him closer. "Then what are you waiting for?"

He touched his lips to hers, and lightning zipped through his veins. Softly exploring, he deepened the kiss, and heard her moan against his mouth. He kissed a trail down her jaw, but she pulled him back again, demanding his lips on hers. When they drew apart, both of them were breathless. He pressed her to him again, not ready to let her go.

"Your hands are cold." He dropped a kiss on her head, not wanting any distance between them.

"I can't imagine why." She drew back slightly and looked up at him. "Who knew woodcarving could lead to that?"

"I didn't." He'd rarely brought women to his woodshop, and though he'd kissed a lot of them, nothing had ever compared to what he'd just shared with Olivia. She quirked an eyebrow at him and he kissed her nose. "It's true. You're a first for me in so many ways, Liv."

Stroking her hair once more, he put his arm around her shoulder to shift their focus back to the table. She was quiet. Was that good or bad?

Before his worry turned into anything bigger, she met his eyes, her lips slightly parted. "I'm so rarely speechless," she said finally.

The woman was like a siren, calling him to temptation. "Do you still want to try carving something?" he asked, trying to tear his gaze away, when all he wanted to do was kiss her again.

She leaned into his side and looked at the table. "Definitely." Moving forward, she put the glove back on and picked up the knife. Using his short tutorial, she began making little cuts and strokes on the wood. "Are you going to do one, too, or just watch me?"

"It's tempting to just watch you," he said, "but maybe I'll do one, too." He picked up some basswood and his second-best knife.

He didn't know what to carve. For so long, he'd carved for calm or simply for the joy of creation. He and Olivia had created something he didn't think he could express through wood. Their relationship had changed him, touched something fundamental inside.

He glanced over at her, watching her concentrate on the block of wood, as if willing it to tell her what she should carve. Maybe he could try to take her mind off of it, so the creativity could flow. "How's work going?"

"Good. Busy. Sam won't let me anywhere near Hannah's case since I have a personal interest. But I did hear through the grapevine that they got some evidence from the car about who her killers are. From the sounds of it, they're building a solid case." She made another cut, and he could see a shape starting to form. A bear, maybe?

Mick started to visualize what his own block of wood could be, a shape that would always remind him of what they'd shared tonight. "An arrest might give some closure to Hannah's parents. Maybe even for Will someday, when he's old enough to understand."

"Her parents have been through so much and still have to get through Hannah's funeral tomorrow." Olivia stopped carving and looked at him. "Were you able to get a substitute? I know Will would want you there."

"It's all taken care of. I definitely want to be there for him." His carving was taking shape quickly now that he knew what he wanted to do with it. Sort of like his relationship with Olivia. Now that he knew what he wanted, he was ready to move forward. Was she? She'd definitely responded to their kiss. But what had it meant to her?

She glanced up from her bear, possibly a penguin, carving, and caught his eye. "You'll always be there for Will, I know that, but I have to wonder, who was there for you?" she asked softly. "Has there ever been anyone?"

He didn't want her to feel pity for him. He'd found people that had shown him respect and concern. "I joined the army and found my family there. They were my brothers, and I had a CO who took a special interest in me. Made sure I knew that success in life took discipline and hard work. No matter what had happened in the past, it didn't have a hold on your future unless you let it." He glanced over at her, wanting her to understand. "And after a lot of counseling, I decided I was going to put the past behind me. I still have good and bad days like everyone else, but more good than bad. It's easier if I'm helping kids, trying to make a difference for someone."

"I feel the same way a lot of the time. When I'm at my worst, trying to make a difference for someone—get justice for them, help them get through a crisis—thinking about making their life better gives me a purpose." She shrugged and bit her lip as if weighing her words. "If you think about it, we're both out saving the world with wood. You can transform a block into something beautiful and I can get justice when that gavel comes down in my favor."

He nudged her shoulder, impressed. "Wow. That was poetic."

They laughed together and pulled the two stools closer to the table so they could comfortably work on their carvings while they talked about their childhood pets, favorite foods, and places they'd traveled. Mick had never been so content talking about himself with someone. He'd never even thought to whittle with anyone but the army buddy who'd taught him how to do it.

She got quiet at the end as she made a few final adjustments. Finally, she held up her creation. "Finished."

He squinted and tilted his head first to the left, then the right. "Is it an otter? Perhaps a flesh-eating pedicure fish?"

She smacked his shoulder with mock indignation. "Why would I carve either of those things?"

He took it out of her hands. "Okay, okay, I can see it's a bird. It's actually pretty good." And it was. She'd done a great beak and attempted to shape the feathers, which could be hard for beginners, but she'd done well. "You might have a hidden talent, but I don't want you getting too comfortable with sharp blades. We have your addiction to think about."

She put the knife down with raised eyebrows and a smile. "You're just jealous I beat you at ax-throwing."

"I still want a rematch." He blew on his creation and held it up. "What do you think?"

It was a small little wood statue, hollowed out in the middle with two intertwined hearts running through it. Olivia gasped. "How did you do that so fast? It's incredible."

He handed it to her, their fingers brushing, and a zing of awareness shot through him. His hands ached to pull her into his arms again, but he focused on his carving. "Sometimes, it just happens. It's as if the wood knows what it wants to be shaped into."

She slipped her arm around him, holding his carving up to the light. "I can see what you mean about a part of you in every piece that you make. And I hope that one of those hearts in this carving is mine."

"If you want it to be." He bent down, and his lips found hers as if they were his magnetic north. Her thumbs caressed his jaw, then she reached further to sink her fingers into his hair. He leaned against the wood table for support, taking on more of her weight and pulling her closer. After a heart-pounding moment, she drew back, holding her fingers to her lips.

"I better get home if I'm going to get to work early so I can go to the funeral." She gave him a little smile before she stood and let her hand trail across his shoulders. "At least, that's what I *should* do."

He caressed her arm, already looking forward to being with her tomorrow and having her by his side. "What do you *want* to do?"

Her gaze traveled over his face, and she breathed in slowly. "Spend more time with you. Kiss you some more. But sometimes you have to remember what you should do instead of what you want to do."

"If it means I get to see you tomorrow, then I'm all for it." He stood as well, keeping his eyes on hers, wanting her to see his sincerity—to both feel and hear what he was about to say. "I care about you, Olivia. More than I ever thought possible."

She raised up on her tiptoes and kissed him hard. "Thanks for trusting me," she said softly. "It's the greatest gift anyone's ever given me."

Worry crawled up his spine, but he pasted on a smile. She hadn't said she cared for him, just thanked him for his trust. Did that mean something? He held her hand a little tighter as they walked to the car, all of his senses attuned to the woman beside him. He was falling in love with her. His entire life had been centered around a promise he'd made never to love anyone again, never to give anyone power to hurt him beyond bearing. Olivia had changed all that, but if she didn't return his feelings, none of that would matter, she'd walk away.

Once they'd said their goodbyes, he stood on the sidewalk and watched her drive down the street. The moment was like a loop on repeat through his head. He'd been left so many times. Would Olivia be another one to leave him?

Take it a step at a time. They shared something special and she'd felt the connection as strongly as he had. Now he just had to remind himself of that fact, for as long as it took to convince his mind to take a chance and trust his heart.

One step at a time.

CHAPTER EIGHTEEN

Olivia had been so honored when Will asked her and Mick to sit in the front pew with him, his grandparents, and his foster parents. His reddened eyes showed how hard this was for him, but he was trying to be brave. The chapel wasn't large and only three rows had been filled with mourners gathered for Hannah's service. The stained glass window at the front scattered colored light over the white casket, giving it an other-worldly look. A large spray of pink roses draped the casket, and, combined with the other bouquets and the warmth of the church, made the flowers' scent a bit overpowering.

Olivia stared at the picture of Hannah perched atop the casket. It was obviously an older picture, showing a smiling Hannah with a radiance about her, a girl who didn't have a care in the world. The woman Olivia had known had seen and done too much to have any light left in her smile. It was salt in the tender wound that the sweet girl in the picture had gone down a path that had cost her life.

She leaned forward and looked at Will in the middle of the row. He was gazing at the picture with visible tearstains on his cheeks. Her heart ached for him. Wendy's arm had been around his shoulders from the moment they walked into the church, and it was obvious he was comforted by her presence. She was amazing with him.

The short service began with a sermon on the healing power of love. Mick reached over and took her hand. That gesture seemed so natural between them now, a testament to how far they'd come. It also proved the pastor's words true—love could heal. Mick had struggled with his demons from the past, just as she'd had to cope with darkness from the cases she tried, but they'd both tamed them together, the love and caring growing between them making each stronger.

The service wasn't long, and when the organist began to play the postlude music, they stood as the pallbearers gathered and the casket was taken to the waiting hearse.

Hannah's mother approached their little group, and bent down to address Will. "Would you like to come to the cemetery with Grandpa and me? We can meet everyone there."

Will looked at his grandmother solemnly, then back at Wendy, who nodded and said, "We'll be right behind you."

"Okay, Grandma." He slipped his hand into hers, and they walked outside together.

Mick was watching them with a concerned look on his face. Olivia slid her arm around his waist. "Are you okay?"

He nodded and kissed her temple. "I'm glad you're here. How do you think Will's doing?"

"I think he's doing fine. Don't you?" She knit her brows together, mentally going over her impressions of Will today.

She hadn't seen anything unusual, just a little boy grieving for his mother.

"I thought so, but needed a second opinion." He folded the memorial program and slipped it into his pocket. "Will you ride with me to the cemetery?"

"Yes." She wanted to stay close to Mick and Will today. Not that she was worried, but funerals were always emotional touchstones, that sometimes brought unexpected feelings to the surface. If either of them needed her strength, she wanted to be near enough to provide it. "I thought it was a beautiful service."

"I hope Hannah really did find healing and peace like the pastor said." He kept Olivia close on the way to the door. "I want to believe that. And hopefully that thought gave Will something to hold onto as well."

"I'm sure it will." She matched her footsteps to Mick's. "With how young he is, he'll mostly remember the feelings from the day and not much about what was said. He felt loved, I think."

"I hope so. I want that for him."

When they walked to the parking lot, the sun had started to peek through the clouds. Olivia was glad to see it, since the forecast had predicted rain turning to snow later in the day.

Mick opened the passenger door of his car, but before she got in, she gave him a quick kiss on the lips. "And besides remembering how he felt today, he'll remember who was here for him."

He touched her chin with his thumb, his eyes holding her captive. The shadows that had once been in his, had been replaced with the clearer gaze of a man who'd struggled, but was winning the battle. "So will I."

She got in the car, and they drove to the cemetery. The

graveside service was short, but the clouds had cleared, and the sun shone down on the little group of mourners. The rays lit up the area right around her casket, and Will, who stood beside it, as if Hannah was sending them a message of hope that she was going to be watching over her boy.

Will didn't notice. He couldn't keep his eyes off the casket, the tears running down his face. Clutching three roses in his hand, he moved closer to her casket and sobbed, "Mommy. Why did you leave me? Please, please, come back."

Olivia couldn't hold back her own tears at his plea. The tiny niggle of guilt she'd felt ever since the hospital turned into a massive ripple that tore through her emotions. Hannah had left him because Olivia had forced her to run. Maybe if she'd talked to her, instead of calling the police right away, things would have been different. Or if she'd worked harder to get the warrant sooner, she could have had Hannah scooped up before she ran. The guilt settled over her shoulders. If only she'd done her job better, Hannah might be here with her son right now.

Wendy lifted the little boy up in her arms and rocked him back and forth as he cried. His mother was never coming back. His life was forever changed. And Olivia might have prevented that.

They walked back to the car, somber and subdued. Mick held her hand, but she felt empty. What if Will blamed her someday? The thought made her flinch.

"Are you okay?" Mick asked, concern in his eyes.

She nodded, but didn't say anything. Regret mixed with the guilt, pressing down on her, making her lungs ache. What could she say? That Will begging for his mother back had made her feel liable for his loss? Her head knew that wasn't true, but her heart believed it.

They all gathered back at the church where the ladies of the parish put on a luncheon for the family, offering ham, potatoes, and pasta salads, with cookies for dessert. Simple, but appreciated. Hannah's parents stayed near the door, greeting guests, and the hall was mostly quiet except for those few words.

Mick helped Will get a plate and took their place at a table near the front. Olivia took a second to gather her thoughts and stopped to chat with Susan for a minute about the counseling that had been set up for Will. Her thoughts about being at fault were on the tip of her tongue, but Susan was preoccupied with the details of Will's care. Deciding to keep her feelings to herself, Olivia listened to Susan's plans. It was strange how quickly they'd all become attached to Will. He still had an innocence and love for others, despite what he'd been through. So much like Mick.

Olivia smiled as she watched Mick's head so close to Will's, more than likely listening to another soccer statistic. Would Will always be so sweet? When he wanted more answers about his mother's death, could she look him in the eye without any guilt? She wanted to say yes, but couldn't.

After putting a slice of ham and a dollop of mashed potatoes on her plate, Olivia grabbed a fork and napkin, then walked to their table. No matter what was going on inside her head, she didn't want to miss a minute of being with them.

"Wendy told me I can make my own family with anyone I want in it," Will said, his eyes questioning. His tears from earlier had been dried, but he still looked sad. "Is that true?"

Mick glanced at Olivia with a half-smile as she sat down

next to him, then turned back to Will. "I suppose that's true, in a way."

Will hadn't touched the food on the plate in front of him, but had somehow snagged a cookie and clutched it like a lifeline. "Did you make your own family after your mom and dad died?" Will asked Mick before he took a bite.

"I was a lot older than you are when my dad died, so I didn't think I needed a family," Mick said carefully, as if he'd had to think about how to explain his decisions to a little boy. "Hey, weren't you supposed to eat your ham before the cookie?"

Wendy leaned over from the other side of Will. "Yes, he was." She picked up his fork. "Try to eat three bites for me."

"I already had a bite of ham." Will took the fork from her, though. The ham on his plate did have a tiny piece missing. But the discussion of his ham didn't deter him. He went back to questioning Mick, the issue obviously uppermost in his mind. "So you didn't pick anyone to be in a family?"

Mick put his chin in his hand and looked down at him. "No. But if I could have a do-over, I know this really awesome kid who's been teaching me soccer tricks. I'd definitely pick him first."

Will gave him a small smile. "I learned some new tricks to teach you, too. But you can't only have one person in your family. Who else would you have?"

Olivia's lungs squeezed. Would he mention her? Did she want him to? Mick glanced over and she pasted what she hoped was a neutral look on her face. She didn't even dare so much as quirk an eyebrow, waiting to see how he'd handle the question.

He slid his chair back and took her hand, automatically

enveloping hers with his warmth. "Well, I'd want to have Olivia. She'd probably be my tied-for-first pick with you."

A little thrill shot through her. She wanted to cheer. Kiss him. Throw her arms around his neck. But she sat perfectly still in her seat at the table. When she'd won her first court case, she'd been relieved and overjoyed, but still had to maintain a professional demeanor. Jumping up and cheering would have been out of place, and that was the situation here, as well. She couldn't react to Mick choosing her like she wanted to, but maybe she could show him later.

She smiled at that thought, but the shadow of guilt over Hannah muted her joy. Why hadn't she shared her concerns with Mick? She wanted him to trust her enough to tell her what he was feeling, but when the shoe was on the other foot, she hadn't done it. Trust wasn't a one-way street. Definitely something to examine. Later.

"It sounds like we're picking teams at school or something." She slanted her body toward Mick's so she could see Will better. "I liked to play with the boys at recess, but they always picked me last because I was a girl."

Will screwed up his face, as if trying to make sense of that. "I would have picked you first. Well, if you were fast, anyway." He leaned over Mick and put his face close to hers. "If you could pick a family, who would you pick?"

"Well, I have my mom and dad and my brother Drew. But if I could pick more people to be in my family, I'd definitely want to have you . . ." she hesitated and then plunged on, "and Mick, too." She ruffled his hair, but looked at Mick. His expression was so serious, she wondered if he'd heard her. But then he grinned and her heart tripped over itself. He'd heard. "Who's in your made family, Will?"

He pointed to the entryway. "I still have my grandma and grandpa, but now I have Wendy and Eric, Joseph, and Garret. And you and Mick." He finished with a proud smile. "I made myself a big family."

"Glad I made the cut," Mick said with a laugh, as he drew Will close to his side. "I was worried there for a minute."

"You were?" Will pushed his chair back and threw his arms around Mick's neck with a sniff. "But I love you."

Mick held him tight, and Olivia felt her eyes prick with tears. "I love you, too, buddy," Mick said into Will's ear. "No matter what happens, I'll always be there when you need me."

Will nodded and wiped his eyes. Olivia handed him a napkin and took one for herself. A made family was exactly what Will had. She was happy for him, but sadness still lingered over his loss and her part in it. Should she go back and review her actions? What could she have done better?

She wanted to retreat, to go home and just think, but Drew, Tori, and Cal walked in. Olivia went over to greet them. "I didn't expect to see you here." She leaned in and kissed her brother on the cheek, then hugged Tori and Cal.

"The obituary said that others could come and pay their respects, so here we are. We wanted to support you today." Drew tugged on his tie, which was already crooked. "Looks like we're the first non-family guests here."

"You are. Hannah's parents are saying goodbye to some of their extended family that traveled from Washington for the funeral." Olivia led them over to where they were standing. "Let me introduce you."

Once they'd shaken hands and given condolences, Cal dragged them over to the dessert table. Drew stood next to Tori and surveyed the cookies, but didn't take one. Instead, he turned to Olivia and gave her a hug. "Are you going to tell me what's wrong?"

How could he read her so well? "It's been an emotional day." Olivia glanced back at Will. Eric was handing him another cookie. "Will's been a trooper, though."

"It's got to be so hard for him." Tori held Cal close to her side. "Losing a parent can be so disorienting."

"Mom, can I have a cookie?" Cal asked. The plates were at his eye level, the perfect temptation. When Tori nodded, he walked around the other side to see all the rest of the baked goods.

Tori watched him go with an indulgent smile. "I don't know that Cal has very many memories of his father. They seem to be fading more and more, which is a relief for me since his father was so volatile." Drew put his arm around her, silently offering his support. "But he has an amazing father now."

She gave her husband a tender look, but Olivia didn't feel the twinge of envy that had troubled her before. Happiness swirled through her middle when she thought of her and Mick. Being with him felt like she'd found the person who filled up empty spaces she hadn't even realized she had. At the same time, a whisper of worry had followed her since the cemetery. Why was she hesitating to confide in him? He'd earned her trust.

Drew broke into her thoughts by giving Tori a quick peck on the lips. "We need to find you a seat. I don't want you on your feet too long."

That was an odd thing for him to say. Olivia's brow furrowed. "She's on her feet all day at school. Are you not feeling well, Tori?" She looked between them, their smiles bigger than normal. "What's going on?"

"I wanted to invite you over to the house to tell you, but Drew can't wait." Tori looked over at him and held a hand to her mouth before she glanced at the others in the room, then said quietly, "We're going to have a baby next summer."

"A baby!" Olivia threw her arms around them both in a group hug. "I'm so thrilled for you. I love being an aunt."

Mick came up behind her and slipped an arm around her shoulders. "Hey, looks like I missed something."

Olivia turned, excited to share the news with him. "Drew and Tori are going to have a baby."

"Congratulations." Mick didn't hesitate and stepped forward to shake Drew's hand. "I'm so happy for you two."

Drew gripped Mick's shoulder. "Thanks. I've wanted to apologize for how things went down in the teacher's lounge the other day. I worry about my baby sister a lot, but I've really been impressed with how you've taken Will under your wing."

Olivia groaned as she stepped between the two men and faced her brother. "What happened in the teacher's lounge?"

Drew didn't answer, but quirked his lips into a half-smile as he looked over her head at Mick. "Just so we're clear, I'll still have words with you if you hurt my sister."

Olivia rolled her eyes good-naturedly. "Hey, I'm a kickboxer, remember? I can do more than words."

Mick held up his hands. "Whoa, I can assure both of you that no big brother moves or kickboxing will be necessary." He tugged Olivia to his side. "You can trust me."

"As long as it stays that way." Drew's eyes were on his sister. "I admit, I've never seen you look so happy."

Olivia leaned her head on Mick's shoulder. "I could say the same thing about you."

Will left Wendy's side for the first time all day and crossed the room to Mick. Glancing around at all the adults, he gave Drew a little wave. "My grandma said I should thank everyone for coming," he told them, but his eyes were on the cookie table. Cal was still standing on the other side, trying to decide what cookie to eat. "Maybe I'll go tell that boy over there."

"His name is Cal," Tori offered, as she crouched down to get on Will's eye-level. "And I'm sorry about your mom."

"Me, too." Will held out his hand like he'd seen his grandpa do, and Tori shook it. It was adorable and heartbreaking at the same time.

As soon as he could, Will walked around the dessert table, and the adults watched him thank Cal for coming. It wasn't long before the boys were talking about which cookies tasted the best.

"They do have a few things in common," Tori said, as if she were thinking out loud. "Cal lost his father, and they both love soccer. Maybe we could set up a play date between the two of them. It might help for Will to have someone his own age to play with, and even talk to, if he wants."

"I bet Will would love that. The park is his favorite, besides the soccer field." Mick looked at Olivia, then back at Drew. He squared his shoulders and took a breath, so Olivia knew whatever he was about to say wasn't easy. She tensed. Did she need to get between him and her brother?

"It might be fun to go on a double-date with you and Drew,"

he said to Tori. "Olivia took me to this new axe-throwing place, and I've been wanting a rematch. Then Drew can prove my theory about whether Olivia's being good at everything she tries is a genetic trait or not."

Olivia looked up at him, trying to cover her surprise. He was reaching out to her brother, offering to spend time with him in spite of their differences. Her throat closed, holding back happy tears. She moved closer to Mick. Any misgivings she'd had about the two men being in the same room eased. It was as if Mick knew just what she needed.

Drew looked amused at the date idea, but he didn't dismiss it out of hand. "Let me get this straight. If I'm not good at axe-throwing, then her skill isn't genetic?"

"That's my theory," Mick said as he met Olivia's eyes. "She claims she'd never thrown an axe before, but she was like a pro."

Drew rubbed his chin. "To tell you the truth, I'm a little surprised she beat you. Don't you work with knives and wood all day? I thought you'd have an affinity for stuff like that."

"He wasn't bad," Olivia put in. "Just had a little too much spin on his throw. Needed a softer touch." She shivered, remembering how he'd claimed his soft touch and nearly kissed her in the middle of the axe-throwing range.

He must have felt her shiver and mistaken it for being cold. Moving away slightly, he shrugged out of his suit jacket and placed it around her shoulders. She didn't protest the thoughtful gesture and just pulled the jacket closer around her, breathing in his spicy, clean scent.

He began to unbutton the cuffs of his dress shirt and roll them to his elbows. "You've got a point, there, Dalton," he said to Drew. "Maybe I'll make some targets and practice. I'd hate to have to turn in my man card, or woodsman card, or whatever it is I'm supposed to have."

"Maybe I could help," Olivia offered, a mischievous look in her eye. She wouldn't mind another trip to his wood shop and a lesson in woodworking.

Mick gave her a wicked grin, and she knew her thoughts were mirroring his. "That's another thing you were really good at." He glanced at Drew. "Did you know your sister has a talent for bird carving?"

"Mick's a great teacher," she said, but her thoughts were on how she'd felt in his arms and how easily they'd chatted about their lives. Comfortable and connected—that was the perfect way to describe it. But she needed to talk to him about Will and Hannah and her feeling of responsibility. She didn't want any secrets between them anymore.

"All right, you two, I don't want to hear about what Mick is teaching you. Go get a cookie or something," Drew said, waving toward the dessert table.

"I'd love to. Shall we?" Mick curved his arm around Olivia's shoulder, and she matched her stride to his as they walked to the end of the cookie table. Cal and Will were chattering excitedly about soccer tricks and ignored the adults around them. Olivia smiled at how normal everything seemed, even with all that had happened.

"It amazes me how resilient kids are," she murmured, as she picked up a sugar cookie.

"Is everything okay? Something seems off with you." He turned her to face him and pulled his suit jacket closer around her shoulders.

He'd noticed. She tried to stem the sudden tears at how

important that made her feel. He was concerned for her. One more piece of evidence that she could count on him. Trust him.

"I just . . . When I heard Will beg for his mother to come back, I thought maybe if I hadn't cornered her, she wouldn't have run. Or maybe I should have pushed harder for the warrant." Tears started to leak out of her eyes. "What if he blames me someday?"

Mick stared down at her, then drew her into his arms. "You aren't responsible for Hannah's choices. At all. She was ruled by her addiction. Who knows what would have happened to her or Will if you hadn't found her when you did." He kissed the top of her head. "He won't blame you. No one will."

She snuggled closer, letting the steady beat of his heart sound in her ear. It was calming. "I love that little boy. If I could take his pain away, I would."

"Which is why you're feeling guilty. But don't let guilt be your focus. You did your job and the consequences were because of Hannah's choices." He tilted her chin up. "Okay?"

She sniffed. It might not have seemed like a big deal to anyone else, but he hadn't made her feel small. "Thank you." Glancing around to make sure no one was looking, she stood on tiptoe to kiss his cheek. "You inspire me, do you know that?"

He didn't bother to look around before kissing her thoroughly on the lips. "The feeling's mutual."

In his arms, with his reassurances ringing in her ears, Olivia felt like she could conquer anything. Happiness filled her as she stood there with her "made" family nearby, both new and old.

Life was good.

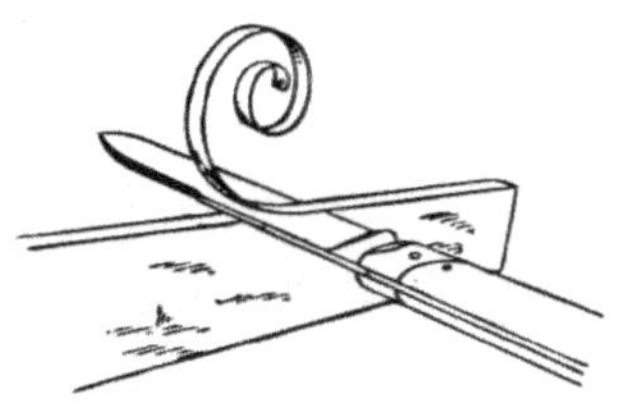

CHAPTER NINETEEN

Mick finished making his last round before class ended, encouraging his little woodworkers-in-the-making. He made it to his own table just as the bell rang. Students crowded around him, laughing and talking about their weekend plans. Mick couldn't hide his happiness, joking right along with them, back to his old teacher self.

"Hey, Mr. Donovan, are you going to Winterfest tomorrow over in Park Valley? I heard they're doing the Polar Plunge again this year." Ethan pushed his long hair out of his eyes as he grinned at Mick. "You up for it? I'd pay to see you in a freezing dunk tank."

"I haven't thought about it. We'll see." Mick knew Ethan was a hardcore winter sports enthusiast and would probably live in a snow cave if his mother would let him. "What about you?"

"I'll be first in line," Ethan said with another wide grin, as he hefted his backpack and headed toward the door. "See you there."

Mick ushered everyone out, reminding them it was Friday and they had to have better plans than hanging out in the woods room. Students slowly trickled into the hall. Mick finally faced his empty classroom. Somehow the projects perched on the shelves always seemed a little sad-looking when the kids were gone. As if the energy the students brought with them transferred to their projects while they were here, but didn't stay when they left.

Mick straightened a few projects on the shelf, then started his cleaning, making sure the knives were in their safety sheaths and the tools were put away. His thoughts drifted to his conversation with Ethan. Mick had been so preoccupied, he'd forgotten about Winterfest tomorrow. Park Valley was the next city over, a ski town that hosted a huge party to kick off the ski season. There were booths from businesses throughout the area, and food, including Rosie's famous scones and jam. The city loved having an event that shouted to the world that the slopes would be open the next day. Park Valley was crowded in the winter with its proximity to some of the greatest skiing in Utah and Lincoln had always benefited from their overflow of tourists, snowboarders and skiers.

Mick didn't ski much—he preferred snowshoeing—but he wanted to ask Olivia if she did. There were so many things he still wanted to discover about her. If he had to guess, he'd say she liked the outdoors as much as he did. He hoped so, anyway. With all the canyons nearby, they could easily spend a hundred dates in them, but if she didn't enjoy being out in the cold, well, he could think of other fun things to do on dates in the winter. As long as they were together, it would be fun.

He grabbed his broom and dustpan to sweep up the

sawdust. Just as he bent over to get the little pile he'd made, he heard his door open. "Hang on a minute," he called over his shoulder.

He straightened only to see Karissa. When they'd dated years ago, she'd come to his room after school a lot, but she hadn't been down here in a long time. He gave her a polite smile as he emptied his dustpan in the trash. "Hey, Karissa."

She walked further into the room and looked around. Mick waited, trying not to feel like he was being inspected.

"Not much has changed in here," she finally said as she lifted a shoulder in a half-shrug and brought her gaze back to him.

Mick took in the new saws and equipment he'd worked hard to get a grant for lining the edges of the room, at the rows of new projects on the shelves—all speaking to him about how things had changed. He didn't bother to point any of that out.

"What can I do for you?" The last time they'd spoken, she'd wanted to ask if the rumors about him were true. Hopefully she wasn't here to do that again. Or ask him any questions about Olivia and Will.

She pulled up a stool and sat down at his work table. Mick raised his eyebrows. Apparently, she intended this to be a long conversation. In the past, all of her long conversations had been about Drew Dalton, but surely she'd moved on now.

"I've been thinking about you ever since you and Drew had words in the teacher's lounge," she said, sweeping a little bit of leftover sawdust on the table into a pile with her hand. "I know it's none of my business, but I was worried."

He pushed up his sleeves and sat down beside her. Was this really about him, or was it more about her feelings for Drew? "Everything's fine. You know how it is when it comes to Drew's sister. He's overprotective. But Olivia and I have worked it out with him."

She pinched her lips together and shook her head. "It's not that Drew's overprotective, really. It's just that after his first wife died, he held his loved ones as close as he could. That's not necessarily a bad thing."

"A little too close if you ask me." He swiped her little sawdust pile into his hand and stood to throw it away. "Did you really come down here to talk about Drew?" Everyone knew Karissa had loved him since high school, but after Drew's marriage to Tori, she'd seemed to be moving on. Or so he'd thought.

"No. I came to talk about you. How did you work it out with Drew? I can't imagine that was easy." She scrunched up her face. "You're right. There I go, talking about Drew again. It's like he's a habit I can't break."

Mick sat back down and gave her a sympathetic pat on her arm. "I get it, and I'm sorry. No one knows more than I do how complicated relationships can be. I never thought I'd find someone like Olivia."

"So you're serious with her?" She flipped her hair over her shoulder and rested her hand on her collarbone. "I was always under the impression that you liked the social part of dating, but weren't looking for commitment."

"It's different with her." He'd heard other people say those words and he'd scoffed at them, but now he understood how true they could be. When she'd confided her fears and guilt to him, it had been like Christmas and opening the gift he was sure wouldn't be under the tree. The strands of trust between them were getting stronger every day, though she hadn't specifically stated her feelings. That detail was worrisome, but he had promised himself not to obsess over it. He was willing to wait. Usually at this point in a relationship he was getting ready to finish up the last few dates and end it. With her, he didn't want it to end. Ever.

Karissa didn't look convinced. She folded her arms and twisted in her chair to face him. "How many dates have you been on?"

He splayed his hands out wide and then relaxed them. "We've only had two official dates, but I've seen her more than that. We've had a lot going on, that's hard to explain."

"Two dates and some extra interactions. Sounds like your normal M.O. to me. When we went out, there were four dates before it was over. How do you know things will be different with her?"

"She makes me want to be better, to reach for things I didn't know I could. I've been stuck in a rut and didn't even know it. She pulled me into a place I'd never thought I'd be." He ran his hands through his hair and wrinkled his nose. "Does that make any sense?"

She let out a sigh. "I understand perfectly. I've been waiting my whole life for that." She let her arm fall to the table. "I've about given up, actually."

"Don't give up. If it can happen to me, it can definitely happen for you."

Karissa laughed and scooted her stool back. "I guess. I always hoped you'd find someone, no matter what you said."

"And I hope you will, too." He stood and pushed his stool in. "Lincoln is such a small town with a limited dating pool. Maybe you need to expand your horizons and date someone from a different county. Look up north or something."

"Actually, I've been thinking about moving away entirely." Karissa stood up, her eyes focusing behind him on the project shelf, rather than on his face. "Get a fresh start."

"Believe me, I understand the feeling, but you'd be missed if you left. You're one of the best teachers here, and a good friend to boot."

"Thanks." She started toward the door, pausing to look at a wooden box with a lid set crookedly on top.

He saw it over her shoulder. "I think we might need to measure a few things again on that project." She laughed and he followed her to the door. "Come down anytime if you want to talk, okay? Door's always open."

"Are you going to the Winterfest tomorrow?" she asked, as she put her hand on the doorknob.

"I'd like to take Olivia. I'm sure she's been before, but there are a few behind-the-scenes places that not everyone knows about." He waggled his eyebrows.

Karissa laughed as she opened the door and stepped into the hall. "Some things never change."

"Maybe." He chuckled. "See you there, I hope."

"We'll see. I do like looking at all the booths." She started down the hall toward the stairs that would lead her to her own classroom. "Good luck. I hope this thing with Olivia works out how you want it to."

So did he. Mick waved as she left and went back in to finish cleaning up, deciding whether to call Olivia and hope she wasn't busy, or head home and wait for her call. With her job, she could be right in the middle of court or sitting at her desk. Would she welcome an interruption?

Looking at his watch, he decided to wait to call her, but he wasn't ready to go home just yet. He walked over to his scrap container where he found two cubes of hardwood, sitting on the top. They looked as if they'd been deliberately placed there, waiting for him to pick them up. Mick turned them over in his hand, thinking how perfect they'd be for a cartouche heart.

He'd always wanted to try making one and was fascinated by the process of having a piece of wood shaped into a long oval, but when it was twisted with just the right amount of pressure, it turned into the shape of a heart. The cartouche heart was such a small project, but maybe since he had a little bit of time before he could possibly talk to or even see Olivia, he should try.

After an hour, he'd gotten to the point of having everything measured and cut, and Mick was starting to sand the edges. It was turning out better than he'd thought and he was excited to show Olivia. If he worked on it a little more tonight, he could definitely have it ready before Winterfest tomorrow. He couldn't wait to see her face when he gave it to her.

His stomach rumbled and he knew it was time to go home. Just as he was locking up, his phone rang, and he smiled when he saw the Caller ID. "Hey, there."

"Hey, stranger," Olivia said. Her voice sounded like she was right next to him. He wished she was. "Did I catch you at a bad time?"

"No, I'm headed home." He walked through the empty halls, glad he had a bit of privacy. That would never happen during school hours. "I was going to try calling you earlier, but didn't want to interrupt if you were in the middle of something. Are you still at work?" Despite her warm tone, he could hear a tired edge to her words. Had she taken any breaks today? Had she eaten?

"I'll still be here for a couple of hours. I was in court until late today and it's been a long, exhausting afternoon. The only thing keeping me going is the thought that maybe you're free tonight and can come relax and have dinner at my place. What do you say?"

Her voice had dropped, and he could hear other people in the background. Was she at the courthouse right now on some sort of recess? Or had a bunch of people suddenly walked into her office? Whatever was going on, he knew she probably didn't have much longer to talk.

"Why don't I come over and make you dinner? You sound like you could use a little pampering." He switched the phone to his other ear as he exited and headed for the parking lot, running through his repertoire of meals he could make that were simple, but still really good.

"You cook?" She let out a soft moan, as if that was the best news she'd ever heard. "Okay, you get major brownie points for that. I should be home around seven. Is that too late?"

"Not at all. That'll give me some time to grab a few things from the store." He gripped the phone tighter. "Has it been the kind of day where we'll eat and then need to watch *Top Gun*?" He'd never forget the pain on her face when she'd told him the real reason she'd watched that movie so many times. If he needed to, he'd watch it with her every day from now on.

"No, not a *Top Gun* day. Maybe a dinner-and-great-conversation-so-I-can-leave-work-behind-kind-of-day, though." Her voice was lighter and his heart lifted.

"I don't know if I can provide the great conversation, but I'll try. Text me your address and I'll meet you there." He decided to go with a lemon and rosemary chicken— just the thing to help combat a tough day.

"I can't wait to see you," she said. The tired edge he'd heard earlier was fading.

"Me or my food?" he teased.

"Both." The roar in the background got louder, and Olivia sighed. "I've got to go. See you soon."

They disconnected, and Mick looked down at his phone with what he was sure was a goofy grin. He'd left her side only twenty-four hours ago, but he couldn't wait to see her again. Truly getting to know a woman, her likes and dislikes, was something he'd done on the surface with the other women he'd dated. With Olivia, it was a whole different ballgame. She knew him, even the things he used to be embarrassed about. And she still stayed.

That was everything he'd never hoped for and didn't want to lose. This relationship with Olivia was risky now that his heart was involved, but if it turned out how he hoped, it would be worth it.

At least, that's what he was counting on.

CHAPTER TWENTY

Olivia was trying to be methodical as she gathered the files she would need to prepare for her cases tomorrow. She was on auto-pilot, because her mind kept going back to Mick coming to her house. She'd never invited anyone to her place before. Her dates hadn't made it to that point, and the reality was, Olivia didn't spend a lot of time there herself. When she wasn't at the office, she went there to sleep and occasionally eat, but that was it. She'd hung up a few paintings, but her apartment was pretty bare. What would he think of it? His own house was warm and cozy, his woodshop filled with his creations. He'd put his heart into the place that he lived. She hadn't.

She stopped going through the files and put her hand on her middle. Did it bother her to have him see how unorganized and bare-bones her home life was? Would he think she was a workaholic?

"He cares more about me than any image I want him to

have," she murmured. He wasn't David, who tried to fit her into a pre-determined box of how he thought she would act. But a part of her was still nervous that he'd be disappointed.

He's making me dinner, she reminded herself. So far, Olivia hadn't seen any evidence that he had any expectations of her. She was worrying for no reason. Instead, she concentrated on finishing up at the office so she could get home. Mick would be waiting for her, and he was exactly what she needed after today.

Jana leaned against the doorjamb with her arms folded, watching Olivia. Her face was comical with her mouth open, obviously overdoing a look of surprise. "What's his name?"

Olivia looked up and couldn't hold back her grin. "You are too insightful for your own good. How do you do that?"

Jana tapped her fingers on her bicep. "It's a gift. But the signs are pretty clear when my boss is happier than I've ever seen her and rushing around trying to leave the office as quickly as possible, when I usually have to kick her out." She pushed off the doorjamb and walked to Olivia's desk. "You didn't answer my question."

Olivia felt her cheeks heat and she bit her lip. Telling Jana made everything seem more real. "Mick. He's coming over to make me dinner tonight. I've got to be out of here in fifteen minutes."

A slow smile crossed over Jana's face. "Well, let me help you, then." She walked over and started to organize the files on Olivia's desk. "I took a look at the docket tomorrow. You've got a busy day ahead of you. I know I don't have to ask, but you've seemed a bit preoccupied lately, so I'm going to anyway. Are you all prepped, especially for the Olson case?"

"As much as I can be. I'll probably go over a few things again tonight after dinner." Or, if she could convince Mick to stay for a while and talk, if it got too late, she'd go over the Olson file in the morning. She stuffed a few more files into her briefcase to take home. "Am I missing anything?"

Jana took another look at the desk and shook her head. "Not that I can see." She stepped forward and put her hand on Olivia's arm. "We've been working together for a long time, and over the years I've watched you put all your time and effort into being an incredible A.D.A. It worried me, though, because there were times when I could tell you thought something was missing in your life. I'm just so happy that you're making room for love."

Olivia pulled her in and gave her a hug. "You're the best assistant and friend I could have asked for. Thanks for sticking by me and being my biggest cheerleader."

Jana pulled back and reached down to hand her the brief-case. Once the strap was on Olivia's shoulder, Jana shooed her out of the room. "Go have a great time tonight. But not too good a time. You've still got court in the morning."

Olivia laughed and headed out the door. "Thanks for the reminder, *Mom!*"

As she drove home, all the green lights were in her favor. Mick was waiting in his car outside her condo. He smiled and got out when she pulled up. Balancing two sacks of groceries in one hand, he bent to open her door.

She eyed the over-stuffed bags. "Did you invite someone else over? How many people are you feeding?"

Mick grinned sheepishly. "I'm making my specialty. Lemon and rosemary chicken, but just in case you don't like that, I also have a Caesar salad and French bread."

"Sounds delicious. And I like a man who's prepared for every contingency." She unlocked her front door and stepped inside. The sun had gone down, but some lingering rays left an orange glow in her entryway. She flipped on the lights, trying to see the place from his perspective. Her favorite painting of a mountain scene was near the door with an entryway table underneath. Her living room had a nice-sized TV and a comfortable couch and chair. There was a picture of Drew and his family and one of her parents on the wall, but other than that, the only other furnishings were two stacks of file boxes in the corner. She inwardly cringed.

She glanced at Mick, who didn't seem to notice. "Which way to the kitchen?" he asked, his eyes on her and not her condo. "This particular dish needs the perfect blend of spices and a little Mick magic, so I better get started."

She inwardly breathed a sigh of relief at how silly she'd been to think he'd care whether or not she had a lot of pictures or nice furniture. "I wouldn't want to get in the way of any Mick magic. Right through here." She kicked off her shoes and walked down the hall. Turning on more lights, she directed him to put the groceries on the counter. "Just tell me what you need."

"You can be my sous chef." He set the bags down and gave her a side glance with a little smirk. "I'm sure you have a great knife set. Didn't you tell David that one in your purse was made of German steel or something?"

She leaned a hip against the counter and snickered. "I don't know what I was thinking. He could have called my bluff."

"You were so believable. I really thought you were going to pull a knife out of your purse. Were you making up those details? Because if so, I'm totally impressed at your improv skills." Mick finished taking everything out of the bags and started to mix the spices. His comfort level in the kitchen fascinated Olivia. Her father and brother didn't cook unless they had to, and called hot dogs and pork and beans from the can a meal, but from the looks of things, Mick ate well and did it all himself.

"I have this weird ability to recall random details at just the right time. My dad likes a good knife and he's always telling me the features of them as if they're a new truck or something. All those details he'd told me about last time I was home popped into my head." She pointed to her knife block on the counter behind him. "If you need a good knife, my set is right behind you."

Mick added a pinch of lemon zest and another spice to a small plastic bag and gave it two shakes, then held it up to the light as if the spices would tell him whether they were mixed enough. "I don't need the knives, but you will. I brought broccoli to go with the chicken because it has a lot of folate in it, which some say helps generate calm mental energy. Who couldn't use that?"

"Hmm…I've never heard that, but I'll take it." She pulled out her best chopping knife and a cutting board. "Sounds like you know a few random facts yourself."

"I dated a woman once who could recite the health benefits of every food on her plate. Guess I learned a few things." His focus turned to the meat. "Do you have a baking dish?"

Olivia hesitated for a second. If she opened her cupboards, he'd see that her cooking supplies consisted of one pot, one baking dish, and a frying pan, with a few leftover containers.

At least they were put away nicely. "Sure. Let me get that for you."

She opened the cupboard and took the baking dish out. Quickly shutting it, she turned around and nearly bumped into Mick.

"Are you okay?" he asked her. "You seem jumpy."

Her cheeks heated and she clenched the dish in her hands so hard it was a miracle the glass didn't crack. "I guess I'm worried you'll notice my condo is pretty bare," she confessed.

"I thought you were efficient. Or maybe a minimalist. Who needs a lot of stuff, right?" He kissed her on the nose. "Did you really think I'd judge you for that?"

And with those few words, her tension was gone. She could relax. Allowing anyone to get close had always been hard for her, but over the last weeks, she'd let Mick in and trusted him with all the parts of her she'd usually kept hidden. He'd given her the validation she'd needed, and subtly let her know she was accepted just as she was. The realization was like a fifty-pound weight had lifted from her shoulders.

"In the interest of full disclosure, I should probably tell you that I worry about a lot of things." She gave him a rueful smile before she went back to chopping the broccoli.

He pressed his thumbs into the pressure points on the back of her neck and massaged them. "You shouldn't. But I'm happy to help you talk through anything you like."

She leaned forward, barely holding in a moan at how good his massage felt. "Same here. I'm good at talking."

He shifted his hand to her chin and angled her face toward him. "You're good at a lot of things." Dipping his head, he kissed her, slow and undemanding until she melted into his arms. Her mind couldn't think about anything else beyond Mick when he did that.

Mick didn't immediately pull away, but gently rained kisses until he stopped at her ear. "I missed you today."

Warmth turned to heat that pooled in her veins before it rushed through her body and made her heart pound with anticipation. She nuzzled his cheek and let her fingers play with the hair at his nape. "My assistant couldn't believe I was hurrying out of the office. I've been looking forward to seeing you all day, through every case hearing and offense report."

"The clock has never moved so slow for me, either." Reaching behind her, he pulled at the pins in her hair holding the bun in place. Untwisting it, he ran his fingers through the strands. "So soft," he murmured. "I imagined how your hair would feel so many times. I wanted to see it down when you and Drew met us at Rosie's that second time."

Her heart stuttered as his fingers tangled in her hair, and she nearly sagged against the cupboard since her knees wouldn't support her anymore. "Not the first time?"

"You were in full lawyer mode then, so you were a little daunting to think of in any regard except to get out of your way." She gave a low laugh. His eyes moved over her face, and his thumb caressed her bottom lip. "But once you showed me your soft side, I was hooked."

The deep blue of his eyes drew her in, urged her closer. She slid her hands down his chest. "I could say the same about you. When I saw you put your arm around Will that night and put his needs first, you stole my heart."

He looked relieved and for a fleeting moment, Olivia wondered if he hadn't realized that. She stroked his jaw and he leaned down to lightly kiss her forehead, then moved down to kiss both cheeks, and her nose.

"You had my heart from the beginning. I just didn't know it yet." And then he touched his lips to hers.

Olivia couldn't get close enough. She pressed against him, her hands running up his neck to thread through his hair. The fire in her veins radiated out to every nerve ending. She never wanted to let him go.

He broke away to catch his breath, but kept her in the shelter of his body. "I think I'm falling in love with you, Olivia," he whispered. "I've never felt this way about anyone else before."

Her heart sang at his words. This man in front of her was so much more than she'd ever dreamed of. Holding his face in her hands, she looked into his eyes. "I think I fell in love with you when I saw how willing you were to change your life in order to take care of a little boy who needed you."

He kissed her again, soft and sweet, sealing the words they'd said with a promise of a future to cement them. When he drew back, he glanced at the food behind them. "We're going to be eating at midnight at this rate."

"You distracted me," she said with a grin, as she hugged him. "Not that I mind."

He moved away and took the baking dish with him. "Well, if you thought you liked me before, wait until you try my lemon and rosemary chicken."

They got back to work and it didn't take long to get the chicken in the oven, the vegetables chopped and in the steamer, and the salad tossed.

"Let's go into the living room to relax while the food cooks,"

Olivia suggested. *And maybe get some snuggle time on the couch.* "I can't wait for all the great conversation you promised me."

"I said I'd try, but made no promises," he protested with a laugh.

She led him to the other room and claimed a spot in the middle of the couch. Mick sat next to her and pulled her into his arms, kissing her temple. "Tell me about your day."

Olivia relaxed into the warmth of his arms. "I had a closing argument that went really well. I've got to be in court tomorrow again, on a different case. Not much exciting, really." She turned so she could see his face. "Oh, I did hear that they were able to swear out an arrest warrant for Antonio Castillo. They got solid evidence that he was the one who killed Hannah." She shook her head. "He's the second in command over the western U.S. branch of the cartel. We've been after him for years, but he's always managed to wiggle his way out of possible charges. This time, he finally made a mistake."

Mick interlaced his fingers with hers and tucked her close to his side. "Maybe Hannah's death will have some meaning if you can put him away."

Olivia had thought the same thing. No one wanted Hannah's death to be just another statistic on the drug epidemic.

"None of this should ever touch Will, right? I mean, no one from Castillo's cartel will come after him." Mick was obviously worried, and she hurried to reassure him.

"We'll keep some safeguards in place, just in case, but I think he'll be okay. This particular cartel seems more concerned about product and branching into new territories than seeking revenge. I doubt they'll be looking for Will." Olivia laid her head on Mick's chest and put her ear over his heart. This spot was quickly becoming her favorite. "I'm glad we're making some progress in stopping the flow of drugs. It's a losing battle, but every time we chop off an arm, it's motivating enough to keep going to find the rest of the monster."

"I don't envy you your job." He rubbed her arm. "Mine has a few perks, though. The students reminded me that tomorrow is Winterfest over in Park Valley. Lots of food and it'll be fun if you come with me. We could go over after dinner, or whenever you get done."

She pulled her legs up and looked at Mick. "Winterfest is one of my favorite things. This year, I'm going to dare Drew to do the Polar Bear Plunge. He's not as adventurous as you might think, but I try to help him break out of his shell."

"Are we talking about the same man? I don't think I would ever use the word *adventurous* in the same sentence as *Drew Dalton*." Mick's laugh rumbled through his chest. She gave him a playful swat and he held up his hands in mock-defense. "But if he does the Plunge, then maybe I'll see him in a new light."

"That could be his incentive, then, to be adventurous in your eyes." Her heart turned over when he smiled, and she couldn't help herself. She reached out to touch that elusive dimple. "What about you? Are you feeling adventurous these days?"

"You know I'm up for almost anything." He rested his chin on the top of her head. "What did you have in mind? Are we finally going to get the fish pedicure?"

She shook her head slowly. "I was hoping you'd come home to meet my parents. This Sunday."

Mick's entire body went very still. The easygoing vibe they'd had a moment ago disappeared when he didn't say anything. Had she scared him off?

"I don't think I've ever met anyone's parents before," he said, musing aloud. "Another first with you."

She squeezed his hand as her heart melted into a puddle in her chest. He'd missed so much happiness in his life when it came to family and genuine connections. "My family is going to love you. Well, at least my parents. Drew might take a little longer to come around."

"You're pretty optimistic about that." He sounded unsure, so she shifted to cradle his face in her hands.

"I know they will. And I think you'll love them, too. They're pretty great. If you know anything about ice-fishing or snow-shoeing, my dad will be your best friend for life." Olivia shivered at the memory of her last winter outing with her dad. "I never could get into ice-fishing. Sitting on the ice for hours, listening for cracks and creaks, hoping you don't fall through. That's not fun to me."

"I love snowshoeing," Mick said, brightening at the mention of it. "I bought a top-of-the-line pair last year that I've been waiting to try out. And there's nothing like a little Mother Nature therapy to help keep you grounded."

"See? You and my dad will get along great. And if you compliment my mom's cooking, she'll love you forever." She pulled him down to her and kissed him lightly on the lips.

"I generally don't date a woman more than four times," he said solemnly. Olivia blinked, surprised at the abrupt topic change. "If we go to Winterfest tomorrow and then to your parents on Sunday . . . we'll have had five dates." He kissed her back and lingered over her lips. "Another first," he murmured.

"I'm liking all these firsts," she said. "And I hope I get a lot more than five dates from you." The timer on the oven dinged, but neither of them moved.

"Didn't you say you liked a little adventure?" He ran his finger down her cheekbone, and a trail of heat stole over her skin. "I think a relationship with me would qualify."

"I'm totally up for the challenge." And then she kissed him again.

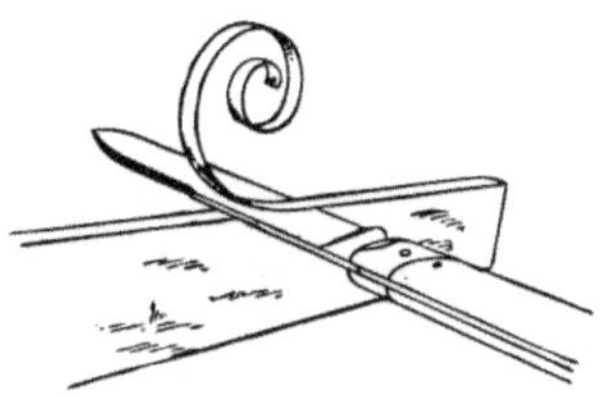

CHAPTER TWENTY-ONE

The Winterfest kickoff always started in the Park Valley town square with a few remarks by the mayor, but this year they also had a ceremonial ribbon-cutting for the new ski-lift on the mountain. Everyone was excited about that, and Mick knew the slopes would be crowded with people tomorrow. The streets of Park Valley, and even Lincoln, were about to get a lot more jam-packed as well, which was the only downside to living here.

Mick took Olivia's hand and pulled her close to the fountain in the middle of the town square. The fountain's top three tiers boasted a large sculpted set of skiers, which was appropriate, but not something you saw on a fountain every day. For the celebration, the entire fountain was lit up with lights, and they twinkled softly as Mick sat on a bench in front of it and drew Olivia down with him.

"I want to give you something," he said, as he rubbed the

cartouche heart in his pocket. He wasn't nervous at all, which was another first for him. This was everything he'd been dreaming of lately.

Her eyes were luminous in the moonlight. Her hair was down, framing her face. Mick could barely resist pulling her to him for a kiss.

"What is it?" she asked, looking at him expectantly.

Mick pulled it out of his pocket and showed it to her. "It's a cartouche heart that I made into a necklace," he explained.

Olivia took the cartouche from him and studied it. Turning it over, she used both hands to press on different points of the flat surface and was rewarded when it slid into its heart shape. "Amazing." She reached up and touched his jaw, pulling him to her for a kiss. "Thank you."

"I wasn't sure if you'd know what it did," he said when they drew apart.

"I watched the *Illusionist* movie a few years back and loved the scene with the locket." She fiddled with the clasp. "Will you help me put it on?"

"Sure," he murmured, as he moved her hair to the side so he could do up the clasp. When he was finished, he softly kissed the nape of her neck, glad he'd thought of the idea of adding a chain so she could wear it. "It's symbolic," he said in her ear, loving her little shivers when he did that. He pulled her against him. "We were just two ordinary people, going along," he started.

"And then, with a little unexpected twist, my heart is in your hands, and I don't want it back." She turned to face him, her fingers rubbing the heart nestled at her throat. "I love you, Mick."

"I love you, too." They stood there in the middle of the square, and Mick bent his head, kissing her until they were both breathless. He stroked her hair, the once-dark recesses in his soul lit up with her warmth and light.

They held hands and walked slowly toward the booths. There were new ones they weren't familiar with, but as they continued down the sidewalk, they saw some booth owners they knew. Bea waved to them, but didn't stop her sales pitch to a young couple holding up a ski parka to the light. Jake was there with his little girl at his side, running a wheel of chance to have a free limousine and chauffeur for a night. Mick needed to go in and look at Jake's inventory for cars now that his Mustang was totaled. He still needed to call his insurance company back. But he wanted to get to know Jake better, especially after his offer to be there for him if he needed anything as one father to another. Lincoln had sometimes felt like a too-small town that always had a lot of rumors going around, but he'd really seen the goodness in people when he'd needed it.

Olivia drifted toward Rosie's booth, where they could smell the scones and jam from fifty paces out. The line was a little long, but not too bad, so they headed to the back of it. A woman with bright red hair stepped forward and put her hand on Mick's arm. "Hey, Mick, I haven't seen you around for a while."

He looked down at Noelle, a waitress he'd dated about six months ago. "Oh, hey." He turned and drew Olivia closer. "Let me introduce you to the reason I haven't been around."

Olivia smiled and greeted the other woman. Noelle was friendly and moved to Olivia's side. "Next time you two come into Rosie's, we should sit down and catch up. I want to hear how you finally took this guy off the market."

Mick felt a flush creep up his neck. "It's not a very interesting story," he said as he steered Olivia toward the back of the line.

"I doubt that," Noelle called as they walked away, but before they were out of earshot.

Several people gave them curious glances as they passed others waiting in line, but Olivia just laughed at his obvious embarrassment. "She seems nice."

He stopped when they were near the end and rolled his eyes. "I don't want to talk about Noelle. Or anyone else, actually. I want to make plans for the rest of the weekend with you."

Olivia looked back at Noelle. "She didn't seem jealous or upset to see you with me."

Mick furrowed his brow, but followed her gaze. "Why would she?"

"Exes aren't generally happy to see a former boyfriend move on." Olivia nudged Mick to the back of the line and stood next to him. "But I didn't get that vibe from her."

Mick turned and hugged her. "Like I said, the women I dated had no expectations. We went on fun dates, but there was always an end in sight."

Olivia cuddled closer, and he tucked the top of her head under his chin. She seemed so surprised that Noelle had been nice to her when he couldn't imagine anyone he'd dated being upset. Well, okay, maybe one or two, but they didn't live nearby, and the chance of them meeting Olivia was slim.

She pulled away slightly to look at him. "Even though those other women didn't have expectations, I hope you don't mind if I have a few." She gave him a mischievous smile, and he couldn't resist leaning down to press his lips against hers.

The simmering arc of energy between them immediately leapt to life, and he angled her head so he'd have better access to her lips. The festival faded away until there was only her warmth against him, the shadows he'd carried for so long lighter in the strength of their love.

When they came up for air, there was a round of applause, some cheers, and catcalls. Mont and Janice had lined up behind them and were staring, their mouths open. Mick hoped Janice would be sure to tell everyone in town about the kiss if they hadn't witnessed it for themselves. He smiled broadly as Olivia self-consciously buried her face in his neck. From the front of the line, Karissa and Mrs. Eliason held up their hot chocolate cups in a toast.

"Can we come back for scones later?" Olivia asked, peeking around at the crowd. "Much later."

"Are you embarrassed?" Mick chuckled, as they turned around and walked toward another booth. "Do ADA's not usually indulge in PDA?"

Olivia laughed. "Let's put it this way. PDA has been MIA in this ADA's life, but she could get used to it PDQ. How's that?"

She never failed to impress him. "I'm always at your service if you want to practice getting used to PDA," he said with a wink.

They strolled toward the outskirts of the town square, near the entrance to the booth area. The wind had died down from earlier, and though it was still cold, the weather was perfect for the festival.

"There's Wendy and Eric and the boys." Mick pointed out the shadowy figures that were just coming into the lighted area.

They were walking straight toward them, Will in the middle of his two foster brothers.

Olivia stood on tiptoe and kissed Mick one more time. "Just practicing," she said with a grin. "And to warm up my lips."

"You don't need an excuse." Mick looked around and bent for another quick peck. "I'm a willing accomplice."

They laughed and jumped a bit when they noticed Will was suddenly at their elbows. He pulled his hat down over his ears and looked up at them. "I saw you kissing," he said by way of greeting. His nose crinkled. "It was gross."

Mick held in a smile. *Gross* was the last word he'd use to describe kissing Olivia, but to a seven-year-old, girls weren't all that interesting yet. He decided to change the subject.

"How have you been?" Mick asked, kneeling down to zip Will's coat up the rest of the way.

"Great. I got to be Student of the Day today. And my grandma and grandpa are coming to see me tomorrow." Will pulled the zipper back down. "I get hot if it's zipped up the whole way."

"Still looks good on you, though," Mick said, putting his arm around Will. "I'm glad I picked it out."

"No." Will shook his head. "I picked it out by myself."

"You're right. I remember now. That was the day when I took you to the soccer field and you were a black and red-striped blur running circles around me." Mick squeezed Will's shoulder. "We need to do that again as soon as the weather gets warmer."

"And I need you to draw me another picture." Olivia joined in. She bent down to his level. "I put the first one you drew on my desk, and I've gotten a lot of comments about it. Everyone wants to know all about the artist who drew it. You just might have a career as an artist instead of a soccer player."

He wrinkled his nose again, as if that was the worst idea he'd ever heard. "No way. Soccer players make way more money." His foster brothers pointed to the wheel that Jake was spinning for the limousine prize, and they waved Will over. He broke into a grin. "Hey, I gotta go spin the wheel. See you guys later, okay?"

"Stay with your brothers," Wendy called. The oldest one held his hand up to show he'd heard her.

They all chuckled, watching the boys rush off, Will just a few steps behind his foster brothers. Mick couldn't help but think of the first time he'd met Will—a hungry boy who spent way too much time alone. Things had really changed since then.

"How are things going since the funeral?" Olivia asked Wendy.

"He has his moments, but he's stuck on the idea of making his own family now." Wendy looked over at Eric, who nodded. "We haven't mentioned anything to Will yet, but we've been talking about adoption."

Eric turned to Mick. "I know you're close, but we'd like to have your support. He fits so well in our family, it feels like he was always meant to be there."

Mick felt a twinge of sadness, not for Will, but for himself. "I knew you guys were the right fit for him from the beginning." He shifted so he could see Will spinning the wheel. "Maybe I can be like the cool uncle."

Olivia hugged Wendy. "It's a wonderful idea and you know I'll do anything I can to help."

Wendy stepped back, beaming. "Thank you. We've really grown to love that little guy."

"He's easy to love." Mick had thought his place in Will's life might be as a father, but as soon as Wendy and Eric said adoption, that vision had changed. Seeing him in a family was what was best for Will, he knew that, but they could still be close. Mick would make sure of it.

All three boys were motioning to Eric and Wendy, so they quickly said their goodbyes and headed over, promising to talk soon.

Mick didn't want to look like he was following them, but wasn't sure what to do next. "Which way do you want to go?" Mick turned Olivia toward the dunk tank. "The Polar Plunge?"

Drew, Tori, and Cal walked up at that moment with steaming cups of hot chocolate in their hands. "I guess you didn't see us waving to you in Rosie's line," Drew said with a shake of his head. "The rest of the town saw you guys, though."

"I don't think they care who was watching." Tori touched Olivia's elbow. "Don't worry, I thought it was romantic. Maybe it'll inspire your brother."

Drew pulled her into his arms and nuzzled her nose. "I'm always happy to kiss you anytime you want."

"Looks like the Daltons are all having a great date night," Olivia commented. "Mick was just talking about heading over to the Polar Plunge dunk tank. Are you up for it this year, Drew?"

"It's not me who needs a dunk in a cold tank. That would be Romeo here, who's been kissing my sister in front of half the town." Drew motioned to Mick with his cup. "Besides, I couldn't leave Tori for that long. Maybe next year."

"Don't use me as an excuse," Tori said, pinching her lips together as if she was suppressing a laugh. "Cal and I will be fine if you want to do the Plunge."

"I heard they're giving out t-shirts this year, Drew," Olivia put in. "You could wear yours with pride to tell everyone you survived the Plunge."

"Sorry, ladies. Not this year." Drew wagged his finger at both of them. "No dare, no threat, not even taunting will get me to leave my wife's side tonight." He lifted his chin and stared down his nose at them to prove his point.

"Another year without a chance to dunk my brother," Olivia said with a mock sigh. "Someday my time will come, though, and I'll be ready." She ignored Drew as he blew out a breath in exasperation. "How are you feeling, Tori?"

Her hand went to her belly, a glow stealing over her face. "I feel great. I don't know if Drew's going to make it, though. I never knew he could take his worrying up a notch."

Olivia gave her brother a teasing look, and her mouth lifted in a knowing smile. "It doesn't seem possible. If this is a girl, though, you're going to have a lot of overprotective daddy to deal with. I don't envy you that."

"I'm right here," Drew grumbled. "And I'm not *that* bad."

They all laughed at his scowl, but he soon joined them with a good-natured chuckle. She leaned in to kiss her brother on the cheek and hug his worries away. "Drew, no matter how much I protest, you are the sweetest brother in the world, and I've always known you have my back, no matter what."

Mick stood in the circle with them, watching and laughing

as they teased Drew. For the first time in memory, Mick didn't feel like an outsider. Olivia was at his side, and Will's words at his mother's funeral came back to him. He had a "made" family now. The one he'd always had a feeling deep down that he wanted and needed, yet didn't know how to look for.

But right here, in this moment, he knew he'd found it.

EPILOGUE

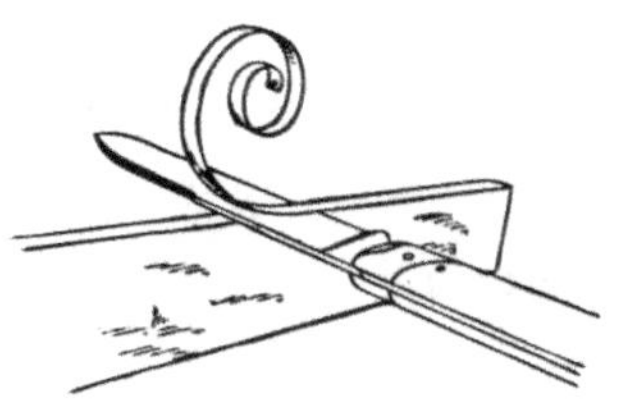

Mick couldn't take his eyes off the judge on the bench in front of him, signing the final adoption papers. Once he was done, Will would officially be part of the Jurgens family. Mick pulled Olivia closer and whispered in her ear. "It's almost a done deal."

She kissed his cheek, her lacy white dress rustling between them. "For both of you."

The last year had brought a lot of changes. Before Eric and Wendy could say anything, Will had asked them to be part of his "made" family. They had petitioned to make it official as soon as they could. Mick and Olivia had been included in their plans from the beginning and today's ceremony was the culmination of months of work.

A lightness spread through his chest as he looked at Will

near the front of the room, his smile as wide as he'd ever seen it. Wendy couldn't stop hugging him as they all watched the judge finish the final bit of paperwork.

"There," he finally said, finishing his last signature with a flourish. Just for fun, he banged his gavel. "All done, young man. You're officially William Jurgens."

Will jumped up and cheered while Eric, Wendy, Joseph, and Garret all whooped and group-hugged him.

"Let's take a picture," Olivia suggested, moving toward them. "Judge Ingersoll, is that okay?"

"Definitely." He came down and smoothed his robes. "And take one with my best side in it, please."

"Of course." Olivia gathered them all together, with the judge and Will in the middle of his new family. She didn't even have to ask anyone to smile. Their faces couldn't have held back their happy grins if they tried.

After a few more pictures, including Will with Mick and Olivia, then some with his grandparents, the judge handed Wendy a folder of papers. She smiled and thanked him one more time before he retired to his chambers.

With a happy sigh, Wendy walked over to Olivia and Mick. She looked Olivia up and down and it didn't seem possible, but her smile got bigger. "Are you ready?"

Olivia held up her diamond engagement ring and it sparkled under the courthouse lights. "As ready as I'm going to be." She raised her eyes to Mick's face and bit her lip.

"I've been ready for months." Mick brought her hand to his mouth and kissed the back of it. "I would have married her the day I asked her."

"Planning a wedding takes a little time, especially for an only daughter," Olivia admonished. "And as my mother has reminded you almost daily since we got engaged, patience is never a bad thing. Anticipation makes the event that much more fun."

"I wouldn't jump right to calling it fun," Mick said, putting his arm around her shoulders. "But I'm willing to wait so you can have the perfect day, especially if it makes my future mother-in-law happy."

"It's definitely going to be a perfect day," Olivia said. "We're at a courthouse which is like my second home, with all the people I love, and I got my favorite judge to marry us."

Will and Eric joined them, and Olivia reached for Will so they could lead the procession down to Judge Daniels court-room, where they'd be having their wedding ceremony. Will readily took her hand, but dragged his feet. "Will I wrinkle your dress if I get too close?"

"I wouldn't care if you did," she assured him, giving him a side-hug. "Do you remember what your job is?"

Will grinned up at her, enfolded in the full skirt of her dress. "Yep. Hand Mick the ring when he tells me it's time."

She smiled. "That's right. You're going to be so good at this best man thing. When your brothers get married, you won't even need to practice."

His little chest puffed up. "It'll be easy." His steps slowed again, and he turned his head to talk to Mick a few paces behind them. "I like that we're both getting all the people we wanted in our 'made' families, just like we said we would. Remember?"

"I sure do." Mick's heart squeezed when he thought back to Will's insistence that they could all make a family. And he'd been right. He'd joined the Jurgens, and Mick and Olivia were about to become man and wife, but the bonds they shared made them all one family. It wasn't traditional by any means, but it worked. "I think it's going to be great that our "made" families have the same anniversary day. We'll always remember them both."

As they turned down another corridor, Drew, Tori, Cal, and baby Sophie were waiting for them in the hall outside a large set of wooden doors. "Judge Daniels is pacing in there, wondering where you are," Drew said as they approached. "She keeps muttering about five minutes early being on time, on time is late, and late is unacceptable."

Olivia took Mick's hand. "We better not keep her waiting then. If she's already talking punctuality, we might be in for a lecture before she'll marry us."

Mick quickened his pace, the thought of anything else getting in the way of his marriage to Olivia making him want to do the Polar Plunge over and over again. "We're only five minutes late. I thought you said learning patience was a good thing."

"Not for a judge, sweetheart." She pulled him toward the judge's chambers, but Mick couldn't tell if the look on her face was worry or nerves. Was she getting cold feet? He tightened his grip on her fingers. At least her hand was warm. That was a good sign.

Mick opened the doors and found the room nearly filled. Olivia's parents were in the front, and her dad gave them a little wave. She'd been right about him. As soon as he found out that Mick loved snowshoeing, they'd become best friends. It had taken most of last winter, but Mick and Mr. Dalton had finally converted the entire family to the sport. Mick had plans to go on at least one more snowshoe trail with Olivia before this winter was over. Maybe when they got back from their honeymoon. Bea had sold them all some snappy red coats that matched Will's, and gloves that matched the coats, although Mick still claimed the privilege of keeping Olivia's hands warm whenever he could.

Drew, Tori, and the kids all took their places beside Mick's almost in-laws and the rest of the Jurgens family sat in the seats right behind them. A few other familiar faces were in the crowd, like Taunya and Jana, but he only had eyes for the woman beside him. From what he could tell, all of their expected guests were here, and the wedding he'd waited months for was about to start.

Mick stood at the back of the room with Olivia's hand resting on the crook of his elbow. He looked down at her. She was radiant, her entire face lit from inside. Her dress wasn't a traditional gown with a long train. Her hem hit mid-calf, but it still had all the lace and satin any bride could want. None of that really mattered to Mick. He only saw her kindness and beauty. He was so lucky she'd agreed to be his wife.

They walked down the aisle toward the judge and any shadows of doubt he might have had melted away. The past year had seen a lot of changes in his life. He and Olivia were now both licensed foster parents. They wanted to do all they could to make a difference for a child in need.

But the biggest change of all was being in love with someone and finding out how compatible you truly were. He'd once thought that Olivia wouldn't want to know the real him, that the ugliness from his childhood had tainted him somehow and would make her want to leave if she saw his weakness. But she'd proven that there was no ugliness in what he'd been through, only the beauty of survival. She was proud of him and loved him. His past would stay where it was, except for the lessons learned, and the future was waiting for them—him and Olivia—and the adventure of a lifetime together.

Just as they reached the judge, Olivia took a step forward, then turned to face Mick. With a grin, she reached out a hand to him, her eyes shining with love. "Do you trust me?"

He didn't hesitate. Taking her hand, he held it over his heart. "Always."

And he meant it.

Dear Reader,

I hope you enjoyed Mick and Olivia's story. I loved seeing how people can change and make room for love in their lives! If you enjoyed the book, I hope you'll leave a review and help other readers find my stories!

The first book in the series, <u>Love's Broken Road</u>, features Drew and Tori's story. If you haven't read it yet, I hope you'll pick it up! I think there will be one more story for the teachers in the small town of Lincoln and I hope you'll watch for that.

If you'd like to be the first to hear about my new releases, get sneak peeks, and see my cover reveals before anyone else AND receive a free book, just sign up for my newsletter on my website www.juliebellon.com

Happy Reading!

Julie

ABOUT THE AUTHOR

Julie Coulter Bellon is the author of over two dozen romantic suspense books and has won several awards, including the coveted RONE award for Best Suspense and a Swoony Award for Best Military Romance. She is also a host on the popular Authors Off the Page podcast.

Julie loves to travel and her favorite cities she's visited so far are probably Athens, Paris, Ottawa, and London. In her free time she loves to read, write, teach, watch Hawaii Five-O reruns, and eat Canadian chocolate. Not necessarily in that order.

If you'd like to be the first to hear about Julie's new projects and receive a free book, you can sign up to be part of her VIP Readers Group at www.juliebellon.com

facebook.com/AuthorJulieCoulterBellon
twitter.com/juliebellon
instagram.com/AuthorJulieCoulterBellon